The Stir Of Echo

Susan Gabriel

ISBN 978-0-9802246-0-3

Published 2007
Re published 2015
Printed by Black Velvet Seductions Publishing
A division of Savage Publications

Visit us at:
www.blackvelvetseductions.com

Dedication

To Sally
Who always believed, even when I didn't. In gratitude and honor of our shared Irish heritage, I dedicate this book to you. May you have warm words on a cold evening, a full moon on a dark night, and a smooth road all the way to your door.

Acknowledgments

Much appreciation to Doug Amtower and Elizabeth Siwek for not disowning me because of what I write; and to Laurie Sanders and Richard Savage for doing what they do so well.

The Homecoming

"Sign and date here, and again, right there. These papers will transfer the title of the house into your name." The attorney offered her a gleaming gold pen. Taking the instrument in her hand, she carefully signed her name on the highlighted areas. The counsel gathered the paperwork, confirming that her signature was affixed to all of the appropriate lines on the document. "Echo," he peered over his tortoiseshell glasses, the corners of his mouth turning up in a half-smile. "That's quite an unusual name. I was wondering if there was a story behind it."

There was that same stupid question again. Echo twirled her carroty locks around her index finger, wishing she had a more interesting answer. The truth was Echo didn't have a clue why she had been saddled with the strange moniker.

"No story, really," Echo replied. "I suppose I should make one up and have it ready for every time someone asks me that very same question."

Echo loved to watch people's expression when she said that. The attorney's confused visage told her that he wasn't certain if he had been insulted or not.

"The truth is, my parents are old hippies, very 'into' planetary alignments and such. I consider myself lucky that they didn't name me something like Spring Rain, or Karma."

The attorney tilted his head to one side, glancing over his spectacles as if she were a piece of prime rib he was sizing up for dinner. "Well, it suits you, somehow."

If you only knew the half of it buddy, Echo thought.

As long as she could recall, Echo had "heard" things; snippets of conversations, ramblings, rants, and whispers. They were echoes from another world, bouncing off of the fabric of time into her ears.

When Echo was a little girl, her Grandmother, a darling but

exceedingly superstitious woman from the old country, urged her not to worry. Gran would tuck her in at night, whispering stories of mythological Celtic gods and the gifts they bestowed on mankind. But Echo knew that it was just a grandmotherly fairy tale designed to quell her fears.

Conventional medicine had provided no answers to her questions. Physically, she was sound as a dollar. In desperation, Echo had visited The Chicago Center for Paranormal Research. There it was confirmed. She was a Clairaudient.

The researcher explained that a clairaudient was a sensitive, gifted with the keen ability to perceive sounds or words from outside sources, such as spirits or other entities. A gift? It felt more like a damned curse.

The messages she received never seemed meant for her, and Echo didn't know how she was supposed to act on them. They were an annoying form of psychic eavesdropping, like conversations overheard in a restaurant—interesting, perhaps, in a voyeuristic way, but soon forgotten.

The purpose of this so-called gift, if there was a purpose, eluded Echo. The researcher advised her that, with diligent training, she would be able to control the communication. Echo had no desire to control anything. She hated making decisions, and right now she hated her life. If she was honest with herself, she would have to admit that she hoped one day the condition would just disappear.

When her parents insisted she take their house in the suburbs, Echo reasoned that she was doing her parents a favor by taking the property off of their hands while they raised their consciousness in far-flung corners of the earth. In fact, she was sure she was subconsciously trying to hide, hoping the voices wouldn't follow her here.

The attorney dropped the keys to her parents' old Victorian into her upturned palm. His fingertips brushed the inside of her wrist. A shiver vibrated through Echo like tiny ripples on a still lake.

"You're dreamin' girl, and you don't even know that you're asleep."

"Excuse me," Echo stammered, "Did you say something?"

"Congratulations. I said congratulations on the house." The attorney leaned over his desktop towards Echo. "Are you alright? You just went a little pale."

The damned voices again; actually, this particular damn voice. It had been haunting her for months.

The attorney stretched his hand across the desk, bringing it to rest on Echo's forearm. "Would you like a drink? I think I have some bourbon stashed around here."

Echo peered through his conservative spectacles into his gray eyes. The attorney's gesture was friendly, almost fatherly. Echo's intuition sensed that it held the promise of more. A vein in her neck pulsed against her throat.

It had been more than a year; sixteen months to be exact, since she had felt the touch of a man. It was not for lack of suitors, for there were many who pursued her. Her celibacy was self-induced.

Average men were bores. Few she met knew how to talk to a woman, much less seduce one. She found them to be unskilled and selfish in the bedroom; laying their full weight on top of her while they pumped away with a predictable rhythm. Sweaty hands roughly kneaded her breasts; sloppy, smothering kisses crushed her tender mouth. Some whimpered like wounded puppies when they climaxed. It wasn't pretty.

Echo wished that one of them, just one, would read a book on the subject, or at least aspire to some form of sexual higher education, but they appeared entirely content, even boastful, of their present skill level. Echo sure as hell wasn't; she wanted more.

Willful and lusty, she had not yet met the man who could handle her. She was born the only child of over-indulgent parents. Some might say that she was spoiled rotten.

Her expectations were high. Finding no man that could live up to them, Echo decided to bench her booty until the right man came along. No sex was better than disappointing sex, she concluded. Besides, she was no stranger to taking care of herself in that department. It wasn't exactly the same, but it helped to keep the horny wolf from her door until she found a suitable mate.

Echo considered the attorney's offer. He was handsome in a suburban sort of way. Neatly trimmed hair, cut into an acceptably short style. A paunch around his middle spoke of hurried meals from fast-food sacks.

Echo scanned the paper-strewn office. Stacks of legal briefs teetered precariously, like paper monuments. Framed diplomas and licenses crookedly lined the walls. Her eyes came to rest on top of a bookcase where plastic sci-fi action figures were arranged in battle.

Oh shit, I'm throwing this one back in the water, she concluded.

Echo withdrew her arm from her counsel's touch, uncrossed her long, lean legs and rose from the chair. A single bead of perspiration crept from beneath her thick curls, slipped down her neck, and then disappeared like a phantom between her breasts.

"Jaysus lass, you are such a dreadful girl!"

That voice again; it seemed to be taunting her, pointing out her faults. In her gut, Echo knew that this voice was not a remnant of an overheard conversation, leaking through the veil of the otherworld; this particular voice was distinctly closer, and it was speaking directly to her.

"I really should be going now. I'd like to get over to the house before dark and get settled in. Thank you for all of your help on this matter." Echo shook hands with the attorney before walking out into the unseasonably warm autumn evening.

The daylight hours were fading. Echo turned her face towards the last rays of the sinking sun and inhaled the dewy air deeply into her lungs. It bore the sweet smell of a new beginning.

* * *

Echo stood in front of her newly acquired Victorian painted lady. Her parents had purchased it only two years before. A stab of guilt cut through her belly. She had never found the time in her schedule to visit her parents here. Now they were off in some foreign land, doing wonderful, altruistic things for mankind, and she was still stuck trying to figure out her place in the world.

Echo was amused by the sweet serenity of the idyllic neighborhood. Leaves glowing with the blush of late September cruised to the pavement like fairy ships on a sea of air and lay scattered along the tree-lined street. Stately, well-kept Victorian homes soared three stories high into the darkening sky, their windows aglow in the twilight.

"Well, this is just like a sappy Thomas Kincade painting," Echo mused aloud.

A gust of wind whistled through the treetops, raining yet more dying leaves onto the bricks.

"It's the perfect place to go unnoticed"

Damn that voice! Would she ever be alone? No matter what she did or where she went, she never had the luxury of privacy.

Okay, whoever you are, please give it a rest. W.E.C.H.O. is signing off for the day, she warned.

The illumination of the street lamp shimmered over the intricate stained glass window on the front door. As Echo turned the lock, a voice with a vague familiarity declared, "Let me be the first to welcome you to the neighborhood."

The voice was not in her ear as it usually was, but came from directly behind her. It had the same distinctive softened vowels and haunting musical lilt as the voice that had attached itself to her in recent days.

Echo whirled around in the direction of the sound. In the shadowy light of the rising crescent moon, she discerned the figure of a man with inky-black hair strolling up the walkway towards her. He was perhaps six foot two in height with broad shoulders that tapered down in a 'V' to a pair of slender hips.

Advancing towards her, he extended his right hand in a cordial gesture. Echo rummaged in her purse for pepper spray.

"Please forgive me, I must have startled you." He stepped into the porch light. "My name is Flynn."

His voice was uncannily similar to the one haunting her. But that was impossible; unless this was a dead man standing on her porch, and he most decidedly did not appear to be a corpse. He was practically the most beautiful specimen of the male species Echo had ever seen.

Indigo eyes peered out from behind thick lashes that were black as a witch's cauldron. A lock of raven hair dangled with careless abandon above his knitted brow. Echo restrained the compulsion to reach out and smooth it back into place with her fingers.

His smile, which tilted to one side, was warm and inviting. It caused Echo to think of rainy afternoons and the things that happen under the covers on those afternoons. A tingling, heavy feeling crept into her pelvis.

"Come on" he said, "I don't bite." He thrust his hand nearer, beseeching her to grasp it.

"Well, girl, are you going to let your neighbor stand here all night with his arm out like he's tryin' to hail a taxi, or are you going to give it a polite shake?"

A neighbor, ah ha, he was a neighbor. Living in the city had made her jumpy. She felt a flush of embarrassment spread across her freckled cheeks. She was grateful for the darkness that concealed the blossoming redness of her fair skin.

Echo grasped his outstretched hand. "Nice to meet you, Flynn. I'm Echo Sullivan." A sense of being protected and secure washed over her as his hand enclosed hers. A fleeting image of his hands exploring her body passed through her brain. *Somebody's horny*, she thought.

"Echo? Isn't that a fine name, and aren't you a lovely lass!" he exclaimed. Pointing towards an expansive, turreted dwelling to his left he explained, "I live in the house four doors down and I was taking a stroll on this glorious evening when I spied you, and thought, now *that* is a lovely lass! So tell me, what is a lovely girl named Echo Sullivan doing in my neighborhood?"

She hadn't been called lass since her grandmother passed away. Was he for real? She just had to ask, "Are you Irish, by any chance?"

"Guilty as charged, I'm afraid. Was it my accent that gave me away or am I smelling of Guinness again?"

He definitely did not smell of Guinness. He smelled like beefcake in a wrapper.

Echo laughed, "No, it was your accent." A bit flustered, she had forgotten the original question. "I'm sorry, what was your first question?"

Echo examined his left hand—no wedding ring. Hmmm, single man, Hollywood good looks, lives in a Victorian…probably gay.

"The neighborhood…you…here," Flynn reminded her.

"Oh, well, my parents own…er, I mean *owned*… this house. They moved out of the country and needed me to take over the mortgage. I needed a change of scenery, and well, here I am, living in post-card U.S.A."

Flynn surveyed the neighborhood. "Yeah, you're right. I guess I never thought of it. It is quite picturesque. I haven't been here that long myself, I just moved in a few months ago."

He had the gift of gab, she had to give him that. Oddly enough, his rambling wasn't bothering her at all. She liked the sound of his voice; in fact, she liked it very much. He was easy on the eyes too, so that made it even more tolerable.

"I had hoped that someone would be movin' in soon. An empty house is not good for property values." He leaned forward whispering. "Drives 'em down, you know. People think the neighborhood might be filled with undesirables when they see a house standing empty for months. You're not one of those undesirable characters, are you?"

Was that a mischievous twinkle glittering in his sapphire blue pools of lust? The glint in his eye made Echo want to look away. It was as if he knew her secrets—as if she had gotten caught with her hand in the cookie jar, or in this case, the nookie jar.

"You appear completely desirable to me," he concluded.

The boldness of his compliment sent up a flirt alert for Echo. Okay, maybe he wasn't gay. She was pretty certain he was coming onto her, and she didn't mind.

"Yes, I mean, no... I guess it all depends on how you look at it. Anyway, I'm just a loner, freelance journalist looking for some peace and quiet. I sort of need to refocus my life, you know; figure out what works and what doesn't work anymore."

She glanced up at the imposing house. "I thought this might be the place to start."

"Well, you've come to the right place. This neighborhood is mostly populated with double income families. They leave for work at the dawn of day and don't return home till sunset. Then it's off to soccer practice, or band practice, or the PTA. All very boring, and full of scheduled activities for the family-minded. I assure you, if it's privacy that you're lookin' for, then this is your destiny. It's the perfect place to go unnoticed."

The perfect place to go unnoticed? She had heard those words spoken just minutes before! Suddenly, feeling very uncomfortable, Echo realized that Flynn still held her hand in his. Awkwardly withdrawing from his grasp, she excused herself. "I should be getting inside and settled in."

"Of course, of course. Nice meeting you, Echo Sullivan. I hope you find your first night in your new home an enjoyable one." Flynn winked at her as if signaling that he knew something she didn't. He waved a casual goodbye over his shoulder as he departed.

Echo assessed him as he walked down the sidewalk, her critical gaze summing up his physique. He was a physically powerful man, perhaps in his late thirties. His dark hair, which he wore slicked back from his forehead, ended in small twists of curls that lightly skimmed the top of his starched, folded collar. He had an exceptionally nice caboose.

His confident stride oozed sensuality. It was almost feline. Echo would not have been surprised to see him spring lithely over a wall, or slink beneath a fence.

Tango dancers in Argentina carried themselves the same way. She recalled gliding across the floor of a Buenos Aires milonga, the tango beat pounding out the rhythm, in the arms of an Argentinian dancer— strong, sure and demanding, leading the dance, asking a question with his body, and she answering him with hers.

Echo's skin prickled with lust.

"If that was the Welcome Wagon, I'm ready to hop on board,"

she muttered. She kept watch until her fascinating new neighbor was enveloped by the lurking shadows.

Bound and determined

Echo stepped into the foyer. Her eyes followed the wide oak staircase that wound its way to the second story as she maneuvered her way around the few boxes that held her personal items, stubbing her toe on the corner of one of the boxes.

"Uggg," Echo grunted, feeling the exhaustion of the day creep into her muscles. "I'll deal with unpacking tomorrow."

Boards creaked beneath her feet as she padded along the hallways inspecting the darkened rooms. The house was eerily quiet; too quiet for Echo's liking.

I'm going to have to get a cat, she thought. The silence around here is deafening.

Despite six months of vacancy, the household appeared as if the previous owner had just stepped out on an errand. Linens, toiletries, pantry items, everything had been left in perfect order.

The kitchen was spacious and bright, much more pleasant than her one bedroom walk-up in the city. She located the necessary items to brew a cup of tea. A cup of tea in a Victorian. How quaint, she chuckled.

In her wildest dreams Echo had never thought she would be living in the 'burbs, and drinking a cup of chamomile tea, but life is a funny thing, she admitted. Giving a little hop, she sat on the counter and raised the cup to her lips. Breathing deeply, she filled her nostrils with the soothing scent of chamomile. She wearily rested the back of her head against the white painted cupboard. Echo allowed her mind to drift; unpacking, changing the utilities to her name, opening a bank account, registering her car, her new neighbor, Flynn. An unconscious grin appeared on her face. Thinking of her hot new neighbor seemed more preferable right now than the other mundane tasks demanding her attention.

She needed to assess him awhile and consider whether or not he was going to be playing the starring role in her next fantasy Jill-off session. She recalled his wry smile and the twinkle in his eye, and the way it caused a guilty, feverish feeling to rush over her. She especially liked the way he said her name, not pronouncing it with a harsh "eh" sound, but drawing it out softly… "Aayko". That could come in handy in a fantasy. He oozed the confidence of a guy who had a big cock and knew how to use it. I wonder if he has a big cock? Hmmm, I'd bet my next paycheck that he does.

Had he been flirting with her or was he just the overly friendly sort? Either way, he'd made a lasting and lust-inspiring impression. Echo recognized a warmth crawling around inside of her that had nothing to do with the chamomile tea.

She started to feel a little neglected. It had been …well, it had been a long time since she'd been laid. Echo squeezed her legs together and wondered what Flynn was like between the sheets.

The wind picked up outside. Barren, skeletal tree branches scratched against the kitchen window like ghostly fingers clawing at the glass. Startled, Echo awoke from her reverie. Placing her empty cup into the sink, she slid off of the countertop and landed with a soft plop on the linoleum floor. The temperature of the room had dropped to a chilly degree. She shivered and chattered her teeth before extinguishing the light.

Briskly rubbing the cold from her arms, she climbed the wide wooden staircase that led to the second story. When she swung open the bathroom door an ancient radiator hissed angrily in the corner. A cavernous claw foot bathtub beckoned.

"Sweet!" she exclaimed. "Let's see if the folks left some candles stashed around here."

Finding a box of candles in the vanity, she turned them over.

"Well, peace, love and understanding," she laughed, "Patchouli!"

Echo lit them, placing them one by one around the room. The earthy aroma wafted in the air. She turned on the tap, testing the water with her fingers. As the bathtub filled with hot water, vapor enveloped the bottom half of the room in a dense fog.

She undressed before the full-length mirror, critiquing herself. She was vain, but had good reason to be. Her ginger hair cascaded in natural waves that tickled the base of her bare shoulder blades.

I could use a trim, she criticized, twisting her body to view the back of her hair. Her legs, lean and toned from years of Yoga practice, stretched up from the floor, and traveled to her firm, rounded bottom. Echo placed her hands on her flat stomach. She blinked at her reflection. The twin pink buds of her C cup breasts stared enticingly back at her.

If nobody loves ya, guess ya gotta love yourself.

Echo lightly circled the palms of her hands over her erect nipples, pausing to tease each with a fingertip.

"I can give you what you don't yet know that you need."

There it was again. The voice, muffled but discernable, rudely interrupting her fantasy.

Really, mused Echo. Unless you can deliver that delicious neighbor of mine into my bed, I seriously doubt that you can give me what I need right now. I'd like a few moments of privacy, so beat it, will ya?

Testing the bathwater with her toes, Echo determined it to be to her liking; not too hot to be uncomfortable, but just temperate enough that she would have to gingerly ease her body into the bathtub.

After acclimating herself to the steamy water, Echo reclined against the cool porcelain. It was time to choreograph her fantasy.

The candles flickered in the moonlit room. Echo squirted viscous drops of perfumed gel, watching them sink into the holes of a yellow sea sponge. Her hands, slick with the syrupy mixture, stroked the sponge leisurely along the length of her neck. Above the waterline, her breasts bobbed buoyantly in the chilly air. Echo massaged the fragrant gel onto her breasts, drifting into a carefully orchestrated fantasy scenario starring her new neighbor, Flynn.

She visualized him standing over her, leering at her in a most lecherous way, his shirt unbuttoned, revealing a sweet six-pack. In her mind's eye, he watched her bathe, telling her what to do and how to do it…and she did each thing he commanded.

"Oh, lovely lass," she imagined him saying, "That's it, touch yourself. Work the soap over your breasts until they glisten."

Echo deposited the sponge into the water and rubbed the slippery gel onto her aching tits with her fingers, kneading them tightly against her chest. Her breasts were magnificent, heavy, round and ultra responsive to touch.

"Very nice," her fantasy Flynn encouraged. "Now show me how you excite those mouthwatering nipples."

Echo rolled her buds between her wet fingers, squeezing and tugging the tightening nubs until they rose from her breasts like firm, pink gumdrops. Echo's hips writhed beneath the water, her buttocks tightening and tilting her pelvis upward in supplication.

This wasn't going to take long. Echo knew her body like a well-read roadmap. She knew the time-saving short cuts as well as the more leisurely scenic routes.

She settled deeper into her vision.

"Hmmm, are you stirring yet? Do you recognize that aching in your pussy?" Flynn prodded. "Search below the water, Echo, to the soft down between your thighs where it's warm and luscious."

Echo glided her hand down her stomach and crawled her fingers over her dewy mound until her fingers encountered the lubricious fluids of her arousal. She envisioned Flynn kneeling near her, his breath tickling her ear as he watched her pleasure herself. His sonorous voice urged her onward.

"Spread your legs. I want a peek at your sweet pussy."

Echo draped her legs widely over each side of the bathtub. Warm, soothing waves of water lapped enticingly at her cunt. In her mind's eye, she conjured the image of Flynn's cock springing to life as she opened her legs for him.

Echo's breath came faster now. Her breasts rose and fell with each deep inhalation of the scented air. She squeezed her eyes tight, her fingers encouraging the blossoming sensations of orgasm. When she traced small circles around her clit, it swelled with delight beneath her touch.

She swiped her folds with her fingertip, picking up more lubrication and swirled the slick juice over her throbbing button until her pussy ached with emptiness. She wished she had unpacked her favorite eight-inch toy, but no matter.

She pushed two fingers of her left hand inside of the dewy folds causing a small, breathless "Oh" to escape from her throat. Savoring the sensation of partial fullness, her strong vaginal muscles tightened around the probing fingers as she worked them deeply into her pussy

In her vision, Flynn stood up and eased his swollen prick into her mouth. It tasted so good. It was huge, too…monstrous. He rocked it in and out of her lips. She matched the imagined rhythm of his thrusting with her fingers. Her legs shuddered and gripped the porcelain, raising her hips. Close, she was so close to orgasmic release. A little more pressure on her craving clit and she would be there.

"Stop! You wicked little vixen, stop that right now! You don't come until I tell you to!"

A draft whistled through the leaky wooden window, extinguishing the candles and leaving Echo in darkness.

Echo opened her eyes, returning to reality. *What the hell? That wasn't supposed to be in my fantasy!*

She pouted in the blackness, the only illumination coming from the glow of the waning moon. She mumbled irritably, "God, I'm pathetic! I can't even Jill-off without being disappointed."

Echo hurled the sea sponge across the bathtub. It split the water's surface, sending foamy droplets splashing onto her face. The spell was broken. Feeling foolish and embarrassed, she pulled her legs inside of the bathtub in defeat.

Later, in the unsettling quiet of her bedroom, she drifted into a restless sleep.

In a deep state of dreaming, she wandered over an unfamiliar land. Drought-cracked earth stretched for miles in every direction. The barren landscape was dotted with the blackened corpses of long-dead trees. As she walked, the crunch and snap of the parched ground crackled in the still air.

With each step, the earth beneath her bare feet crumbled and broke away, falling soundlessly into a dark abyss. Scrambling to stay one step ahead of the crumbling earth, Echo frantically searched the lifeless horizon for a safe haven. Far in the distance, she spotted an immense rock formation, rising from the arid ground like an ancient monument. It stood red against the white-hot sky, its surface jagged and steep as if hewn by some great sword. Its time-worn face seemed solid and secure, strangely out of place in this fragile environment.

Blood pounded in her veins, as she raced with break-neck speed towards the protection of the rock formation, raining clods of pulverized earth into the colorless void.

She didn't dare stop or look back, only pressing onward until breathlessly she flung herself onto the cool, hard surface of the rock base. Clinging to the stone, she looked backward. The path she had run was now a bottomless crevasse that split the earth in two. No matter what lay ahead, she could not go back the same way that she came. Echo pulled herself up to a jagged ledge, the flint-like rock lacerating the tender pads of her fingers. Perhaps if she could get to the top, she might be able to view the land from all angles and find a way out of this horrid place. With resolve and determination, she climbed to the next ledge, and the next.

The sun burned hotly against her fair skin as she searched for footholds on the steep surface. As she ascended, patches of deep green moss sprung up, cooling the soles of her feet. A dense cloud obscured the top of the formation. From here, Echo could feel its misty dampness on her face.

She must be close now. The promise spurred her onward and she found the strength to pull herself onto a smooth outcrop, where she rested for a moment, quenching her parched flesh in the cool vapor of the cloud.

Her eyes searched the endless sky for signs of life…a bird, an insect, anything that would tell her that she was not alone. But the sky only mirrored the emptiness of the landscape below.

Echo examined her hands and knees, scraped and bleeding from her climb, and wondered how she had come to such a forsaken place. If only someone would come along and tell her what to do…which direction to go. But there was only one direction left—up. Echo stood on the ledge, tilted her head skyward and stretched once again, her fingers grasping for a sturdy hold. Finding one that she felt would support her weight, she propelled her body upward, passing through the cloud line, where she found herself standing on the apex of the mountainous boulder.

She sighed with deep relief and satisfaction at having made it to the top. Walking to the opposite edge of the rock, she surveyed the landscape below. Stretched out as far as her eyes could see was a mad scene of utter chaos. There was no order to anything. Abstract structures, with walkways and wings constructed in a willy-nilly fashion, teetered and collapsed beneath their own weight. People wandered aimlessly in every direction. Everyone and everything was acting of its own accord. No one was in control.

Echo shouted out directions and commands to the swarming mass, but her words frustratingly faded into the atmosphere unheeded. She called out for help to no avail. She remained unseen and unheard—solitary and lost.

Far away, across the clouds, the faint call of her name reached her ears. Echo peered in the direction of the sound and noticed a road winding through the sky which hadn't been there before. There was a signpost on the side of the road marked with bizarre symbols. Scratched into the sign was a single word. Tir-na-nog.

"Are you going there?" queried a small voice.

The wispy figure of a woman floated above the rock's surface. Long tresses of white blond hair billowed around the soft features of her pale face. She wore a diaphanous gown of emerald green, which whipped around her in the wind, although Echo could feel no wind at all.

"I …I don't know. I don't know which way to go. I think I'm lost." Echo confessed.

"Well, I have found that if you are lost, it often helps to just wait for someone to direct you."

"How about you…you're here right now." Echo petitioned.

"No, I don't think so. I think it is best if you just wait for someone else."

"What if no one else ever shows up? What if I never get out of this godforsaken place? What if I die here all alone?"

The lady in green laughed, "If, if, if…so many ifs. Balls, said the Queen, if I had 'em I'd be King."

"What in the hell does that mean?"

The green lady clucked her tongue. "Silly girl, it means that sometimes you just have to accept things for what they are, surrender and trust that the universe holds you safely in the palm of its hand."

Leaving Echo with that enigmatic statement, the ethereal lady floated into the distance.

Before she could think on what she had been told, the rock gave way, sending her plummeting into darkness. Deeper and deeper she tumbled into the colorless abyss. She tried to cry out, but no sound emitted from her mouth. Hurtling downward, her descent jerked to an abrupt halt and she found herself suspended in mid-air, face down, her arms and legs splayed apart, held in suspension by iron shackles that encircled her wrists and ankles. She realized that she was nude.

She wanted to go back to the safety of the rock, but it had vanished. Weeping in panic, she thrashed about, wailing at the top of her lungs for help. Her cries bounced back to her across the black horizon. The more vigorously she struggled, the tighter the shackles bit into her flesh. She tried to relax and reason what her next move should be. When she relaxed, she discovered a peacefulness had come over her spirit. At that moment, she realized that the shackles were not elements of punishment; they were instruments for her safety. If they were to vanish, she would plunge headlong into the chasm.

As she willed the terror from her body, submitting to the security of the chains that bound her, a roar, like the sound of a passing train, arose from the depths. A mighty, sultry wind buffeted her naked body. It swirled and moaned, wrapping her skin in sensual sensations. The cyclone licked at her buttocks and fluttered between her legs. It caressed her breasts and tickled her thighs. Her panic subsided as she succumbed to the sensual wind. She hung in the atmosphere, suspended by the restraints, as the zephyr delighted and explored her secret, sensitive places. It was as if a multitude of tempestuous tongues teased and pleasured her flesh until she surrendered to orgasmic release.

Thou Shall Not Covet Thy Neighbor

Flynn paced the floor of his bedroom. From his window, he could see the ginger-haired woman carrying bags of groceries from her car. Chivalry nagged him to rescue her from the burden of the parcels, but he refrained. He had flustered her last night with his bold introduction; it had been a stupid move. You just didn't go around startling women in the dark at their doorway. He considered himself lucky that he avoided a face full of pepper spray.

He should probably take things more slowly, but time was running short. There was so much to do and so few days in which to make it all happen. He had waited longer than his memory could search. He had bided his time for her to be in this precise place at this precise moment in her life. His desire, coupled with the urgency of his business, had caused him to act rashly.

All in all it was a satisfying initial meeting, but something had spooked her near the end. He needed to concoct a plan that would allow him to spend time with her today without scaring her off. He would need an excuse, something not too threatening, and not too flirtatious. It was imperative that he gained her trust. Without that, nothing could go as planned.

Flynn screwed up his courage, tried unsuccessfully to put the disobedient lock of hair back in its proper place on his head, and winked confidently at his reflection in the mirror.

* * *

A mammoth bouquet of hydrangea blossoms greeted Echo as she opened the door.

"Delivery for Miss Sullivan."

The dusty pink and amber of the October blooms obscured the deliverer from Echo's view. Echo was certain they had the wrong house.

"Who are you looking for again? I think you probably have the wrong house."

"No, right house, right girl…these are a housewarming gift."

The deliverer laid the flowers in Echo's arms. Golden rays from the afternoon sun silhouetted the man standing in the doorway. He beamed a sparkling smile in her direction.

"Oh my God, Flynn…you have to be kidding me? I can't believe this. You shouldn't have done… I barely know you." Echo stammered.

"Echo, please, before you go getting your conkers in a knot, it wasn't any big deal. I…uh…well…I sort of nicked them from your garden." Flynn shrugged his shoulders, crinkled his eyes, and raised one eyebrow in a boyish, 'sorry 'bout that'. Echo chuckled to herself. This guy was so adorably smooth he could charm the panties off a Puritan.

"Oh really?" Echo replied. "Well, at least you're an honest thief, if there is such a thing."

"I may be a thief of sorts, but you, girl, have terrible manners," Flynn teased. "This is twice now I have tried to be neighborly and you have left me standin' at the door."

"Well, this is twice that you have taken me by surprise, so I consider us even."

"You have a valid point." Flynn confirmed.

Echo wondered who made him the manners police anyway. "Look, I don't know how it's done in the suburbs, but where I come from women not only do not invite strange men into their homes, they use a triple set of deadbolts to keep them out. I don't mean to be rude…

"No, I was wrong. I'm not as familiar with your country as I should be. I'm not used to being regarded with suspicion. Where I come from, we don't even lock our doors."

"Geez, that must be nice." Echo couldn't imagine a place where they didn't have to be concerned about muggers and rapists and terrorists, or any of the other million and one fears that she had grown accustomed to living with.

Flynn shoved his hands in his pockets, his eyes cast bashfully downward. "I guess I'll just be on my way then. I'm sorry to bother you. You know where I live if you would like to pop over for a cup of tea sometime. The door's always open."

As he turned to leave, Echo realized that she didn't want him to go. He really did seem like a nice guy and, despite his confidence, he appeared sort of lost. He had been so polite and she had acted like the Ugly American.

"Wait," she called out, grasping his elbow. "How about I throw caution to the wind and invite you in for a bit?"

He turned, one eyebrow raised in a questioning look. "No, I don't want to be a pest," he protested. "I'll just take off."

Echo tugged on his elbow, directing him into the doorway. "I insist. Won't you please come in?"

He smiled, his perfect white teeth contrasting sharply against his tanned skin. "If you insist… I'll come in for minute, but I promise I won't stay too long." Flynn had to turn sideways to get through the door so as not to crush the bouquet in her arms.

As he passed, his scent mingled with the sweet, green fragrance of the flowers. He smelled unpolluted and wild, as if he had just emerged from some great forest with the aroma of earth and leaves and pine needles still clinging to his skin. The feminine atmosphere of Echo's house now crackled with testosterone. "Watch your step. Sorry about the boxes," Echo apologized. "I was just starting to unpack them when you knocked. I better put these flowers into some water. Would you like something to drink? An iced tea, maybe… cup of coffee, shot of tequila?"

"Seein' as it's only three in the afternoon, I think I'll opt for the coffee, but you go ahead and have anything you like."

He sure was a sarcastic little bugger.

"Thanks for the permission. Follow me to the kitchen and I'll take care of the flowers and you at the same time."

Echo wanted to thrash herself in the head with the hydrangeas. *What in the hell did I say that for? That sounded like a line straight out of a soap opera. Oh God, he probably thinks I was coming on to him! Just start walking, maybe he didn't catch it.*

As nothing never, ever got past Flynn, he had picked up on her Freudian slip and suppressed a laugh, but could not stifle a mischievous grin.

"In truth," explained Flynn as he took a seat at the yellow kitchen table, "I was thinkin' that perhaps you might be needin' some help unpacking and getting things set right around here. I drive a pretty mean screwdriver when I want to. and I am not bad with heavy lifting either."

"You don't say?" exclaimed Echo, setting the cup of coffee on the table. "Sugar?"

"No trouble at all…darlin'."

For a split second Echo was confused, and then, feeling foolish, she realized that he was teasing her. Why did she act like such an imbecile when this man was around?

"You are quite the kidder, aren't you? Echo goaded. "You know the old saying, that the world can tolerate a dumb-ass but nobody likes a smart-ass. Well, mister smart-ass, you're on. You have just snickered your way into a heap of manual labor."

Flynn sipped his coffee, peeking innocently over the rim of the cup.

"You can finish your coffee, and then come and join me in the foyer. I hope you ate your Wheaties today, because I love to read, and I have lots of boxes of heavy books."

Echo walked out of the kitchen door, calling over her shoulder, "Be careful what you wish for, Flynn…you just might get it!"

* * *

Echo detected his scent before she heard his footsteps in the hallway. Bent over a large carton marked "Bedroom" in fat red marker, she looked up as Flynn walked towards her. He had removed his shirt. The vision of unabashed virility put Echo in a state of suspended animation. Swelling pectoral muscles and wide, brawny shoulders sloped into the flat, undulating surface of his abdomen. A trail of small black hairs began just below his navel and traveled southward, vanishing beneath his belt buckle.

Taken aback by the sight, Echo stared with mouth agape.

Absentmindedly, her hand slackened, releasing a box cutter which fell to the floor, nicking her toe on the way to the ground. A stinging sensation throbbed in her toe, but it could not distract her attention from Flynn's sexy six-pack. "Hope you don't mind, but it's awfully warm today, and that is a new-ish shirt," Flynn implored. Uncharacteristically speechless, Echo stared, spellbound by this specimen of sublime masculinity. "Well, it's white, too," Flynn continued. "You know how hard it is to get a stain out of a white shirt?" Flynn's expression changed to one of surprise. "Oh, Jaysus, you're bleedin'!" He exclaimed.

The urgency of his voice awakened Echo from her daydream. What was he talking about? She followed the direction of his gaze to where a pool of blood was forming under her lacerated foot.

Flynn rushed to her and grabbed her by the elbow, pulling her to her feet. "Come on, come on, girl…let's get a look at that!"

Flynn hoisted Echo up, supporting her on his arm as he led her towards the kitchen. She leaned helplessly against him, feigning a pain that she did not feel, and gripped her hand around his flexed bicep for support. The muscle tightened and rippled beneath her palm. Echo squeezed the dense bulge, testing it for firmness. It was beautifully non-yielding.

His arm encircled her waist and scooped her off her feet, then deposited her atop the kitchen counter.

"Swing your foot up into the sink," Flynn instructed, turning on the water and testing the temperature with his hand.

Echo placed her foot inside of the bowl. Flynn supported her foot in his hand as the water rushed over the laceration. She watched the ribbons of blood, first brilliant red then fading to pink, wash against the white porcelain and swirl in hypnotic arcs down the drain.

No one spoke.

She shifted her gaze to rest on his unclothed form. Her lecherous gaze spellbound, enticed by the droplets of water splashing on his naked chest. She had the urge to lick them, one by delicious one, from his damp flesh.

Flynn leaned his body into hers. Echo closed her eyes, turning her face upwards in anticipation of their lips meeting in a kiss.

"Excuse me there, darlin'," Flynn cooed, "but could you skooch over just a bit so I can reach those paper towels sitting behind you?"

Echo's eyes snapped open. *Oh God, I am such an idiot! Please tell me I did not just do that! I'm behaving like a hormonal teenager!*

Echo scooted to the right and Flynn retrieved the towels, wadding them up and wiping her foot dry. He dabbed at the cut until the blood began to clot.

"There, that should hold it for a second," he said, swiveling her around so her legs dangled off the edge of the counter. Brandishing a finger in front of her face he scolded, "Now you stay here. I will be right back with a bandage."

For a split second, Echo thought he said that he would be right back with a *bondage*. Echo mustered a weak nod.

Flynn dashed off to rummage in the bathroom for first aid supplies.

Echo sat on the edge of the kitchen counter, absentmindedly chewing her fingers in a state of sexual tension. Not only was Flynn the hunkiest man she had ever met, but she was astonished to realize that she really liked him! He made her laugh, he made her think, he was thoughtful, and caring. So far he added up to the total package. She marveled that just the night before she had been sitting in this very same spot fantasizing about this very same fellow, and here he was right now, half-naked, and fixing her boo-boo to boot.

A disembodied female voice boomed into Echo's ears. "This is not a man you will be able to wrap around your finger, Delores!"

That was completely random—and a bit rude, too. Her blood simmered at the unseen interruption of her daydream.

"If I see Delores, whoever that is, I will be sure to tell her," Echo hissed to the ghostly visitor. "You don't have to scream."

Flynn strode into the room proudly displaying mercurochrome, a cotton ball and a roll of white tape. Echo imagined playing doctor with him. She'd like to show him where it hurt.

He stood between Echo's dangling legs, lifting her injured foot to his chest. His skin was comfortingly warm against the sole of her foot. A single drop of blood oozed from the cut and ran down the side of her big toe, sliding onto Flynn's chest.

While Flynn busied himself with bandaging, Echo's eyes followed the path of the blood as it descended his torso. The thick crimson droplet coursed along his stomach, trailing a sticky scarlet ribbon over his rectus abdominus, dipping in and over the rolling hills of his muscles. It veered just to the left of his navel, and then silently disappeared beneath his trousers.

A wave of internal heat caused miniscule beads of perspiration to blossom on her skin.

"There you are. All bandaged...oh, I almost forgot...a kiss it to make it better." Flynn lifted her foot to his lips and placed a kiss on the injured area. Even though his lips only touched the bandage, Echo did feel better, much better.

He lowered her foot. He was standing between her legs, her knees touching his hips. His penetrating gaze honed in on her face, mesmerizing, but unsettling at the same time. What was he staring at her for? Was there something on her face? Echo wiped her cheeks, searching for the offending crumb.

"I have the sudden urge to kiss you," he said. "Would you mind if I kissed you... on the lips?"

On the lips, on the neck, Echo would have allowed his mouth to roam anywhere that he desired.

"Oh, yes," she breathlessly agreed. "I think I'd like that."

Flynn lifted her legs and wrapped them around his hips, drawing her to his body. Before he could press his lips to hers, Echo's mouth lifted to his.

She parted his lips with her tongue and explored his warm, open mouth. Her hands surveyed the anatomy of his back, 'seeing' the outline of his muscles with her fingertips. She felt his heartbeat drumming against her chest and hers pounding a refrain like a million fluttering birds. The dam, which had held back her hunger for so many months, crumbled and released the rising waters of her pent-up passion. She was glad her gauzy prairie skirt veiled the wicked secret of her sodden panties.

Flynn's hands stroked her sides, his thumbs grazing the swell of her breasts enticing Echo's nipples to jut out against her tight-fitting tee. She knew Flynn could feel their hardness brushing his naked flesh, just as she could feel his hardness below, pressing against her pelvis.

Unexpectedly, Flynn put the brakes on. He pulled away, sheepishly dropping his head. "I should go."

Echo had been enjoying the kiss and didn't like it one bit that he had taken his mouth from hers. However, she had to admit that she was a little relieved. If he hadn't stopped, she probably wouldn't have either. Her admiration for Flynn grew. He had to have known that she was willing, and yet he held back. In her opinion, he showed considerable self-control.

She didn't want him leaving on such an awkward and tenuous note.

"No, don't go…please." She wiggled her bandaged toe in his direction. "My foot is banged up. My plans for the day are shot to hell. Let's forget about those boxes and just hang out for a while."

Sliding off of the counter, she lowered her feet to the floor, wincing as she touched the injured foot gingerly to the ground. Flynn reached to steady her, but she waved him off in a display of independence.

"Look, I'm not sure what just happened here, but guess what—I like you. I don't know a single soul in this entire town, and I enjoy your company."

A glimmer of a grin crossed Flynn's face.

Echo's hands seemed to have a mind of their own. She wanted so badly to glide them around his naked waist and caress his flesh with her fingertips. Fearing the compulsion to grope him, she folded her hands in prayerful supplication. "Say that you'll stay for a little while. What am I going to do, all alone in this big house with this bum foot?"

It was so quiet in the room that she could hear the soft scritch scratch of whiskers as Flynn rubbed his chin with his hand in thoughtful contemplation.

"Besides, it *is* your fault that I nearly amputated my toe!" Flynn's eyebrows arched in confusion. "If you hadn't walked in looking like…'" Echo waved a finger up and down his body. "Well, you know…how you look; I would have never dropped that knife."

Flynn's eyes shifted to his shirt which hung guiltily over the back of a chair.

"Another valid point," Flynn conceded. "Alright, you win. I'll keep you company and do my best to keep my knickers on."

* * *

Many hours and three bottles of Pinot Grigio later, the sun had dipped below the horizon, leaving only a trace of a harvest glow in the sky. Echo and Flynn were sprawled like comfortable old friends across the sofa. Both of them being Irish and well in their cups, they fell into a melancholy and reflective mood.

"Ever thought about what you want from your life?" asked Flynn.

Through bleary eyes, Echo drank in the vision of the man sitting next to her. His hair was now a bit unkempt, his body relaxed into the sofa, his long legs stretched for a mile in front of him. He thoughtfully traced the rim of his wine glass with a long, tapered index finger. She was certain that what she wanted most from life at this moment was to pin him to the sofa for an extended snogging session, full of wet kisses and groping hands.

Echo tossed her head back, chuckling. "I know exactly what I want," she exclaimed. But no amount of alcohol could have loosened her tongue enough for her to confess that she wanted to jump his gorgeous bones. She decided, instead, to lighten the mood and hopefully change the subject. Holding her wine glass aloft, she proclaimed, "I want to rule the world!"

"Of course you do." Flynn laughed, the deep rolling sound as infectious as his speech. She had made him laugh. He found her amusing. A warm sensation glowed inside her. She didn't often show her silly side, and it was nice to feel comfortable enough to let it out.

"But, darlin' I'm asking what do you want for yourself...for your soul?"

In emphasis, Flynn placed Echo's hand over her heart.

Echo blinked, trying to better focus her eyes. The touch of his hand on her chest was so warm and tender; it filled Echo with a sentimental emotion. It had been so long since someone had touched her in that way. Now she knew exactly what she wanted from life. Her head buzzed with fuzzy concentration as she struggled to put it into words.

"I suppose that in the end," she began. "I just want to love and be loved...although, I'm not exactly getting my hopes up. Things haven't worked out so well in that department. I hear that I am too picky." Echo paused for a moment, reminiscing over the men in her past. She had drifted through a life of serial monogamy, finding reasons, or perhaps excuses, to discard them all. "Well, maybe I am too picky. But if I already know I'm going to be disappointed, why try anymore at all? Isn't that the definition of insanity; doing the same thing over and over again and expecting a different result? I think I may be ready to go the fuck 'em and forget 'em route. It sure couldn't be any more heart breaking."

Flynn wrapped his arm around Echo's shoulder and snuggled her to his body.

She relaxed into his embrace. She was having trouble keeping her eyes open and it felt as if weights were attached to her lashes, tugging on her lids.

"Don't give up the ghost yet, girl. In the words of John F. Kennedy, 'what's the use of being Irish if the world doesn't break your heart?'"

Wasn't that the damn truth? Echo's throat tightened and burned. Flynn's insightful words had worked their way through her tough exterior and struck at her soft, vulnerable center.

Oh, God, she didn't want to turn into a drunken, blubbering fool in front of him. Fighting the urge to feel sorry for herself, Echo quickly changed the subject. Wiggling her empty wine glass she asked, "Want some more?" and then answered herself. "Thank you, I think I will." Echo sloshed the last of the golden liquid into their goblets.

She had sat up too quickly and now her head swam. *Whoa!* Echo grabbed onto the edge of the coffee table, her hand slapping down sharply on the glass as she tried to regain her coordination. "You are positively circling over Shannon drunk!" hooted Flynn. "This could work to my advantage. Let's see...what'll it be....oh, I know...since you can't hold your liquor like a proper Irishman....

"Wine," she interrupted. "We're drinking wine, not liquor."

Flynn narrowed his eyes. "As I was saying...since you are obviously an amateur Irishman, I challenge you to answer any one question that I ask."

Echo realized that she had gone beyond being tipsy...she was bordering on shit-faced. She put her wine glass on the table, vowing not to drink another drop. She straightened her spine and tried to appear sober.

"Oh, you are an evil, tricky man!" Echo scowled. "Okay, Mister Smarty-Pants, give me your best shot."

"Alright then, and you have to answer it *honestly*...no fairy tales. I want to know your deepest, darkest, most erotic fantasy."

Echo rolled her eyes and set her jaw. *Of all the questions he could have asked, he chose that one!* She doubted he was ready to hear what she had to say.

"You just had to go there, didn't you? I don't know," she hesitated. This was delicate territory. For a moment she considered inventing something because the truth might be too much for him to handle, but, as she tried to concoct a lie, her muddled, wine-soaked brain wouldn't cooperate. There wasn't any way she would be able to weave a believable story in her condition.

"You have to promise not to think that I'm a wanton degenerate. I am going to be honest with you and you can't use it against me later, alright?"

Flynn nodded.

"Promise?" Maybe she could stall him long enough for him to forget what he had asked or maybe he, too, was intoxicated enough not to be shocked...or worse...repulsed.

Flynn covered his heart with his hands, and looked skyward. "I promise on my dearly departed mother, God rest her sainted soul."

"Oh, since you're swearing on your sainted mother, I guess it's okay for me to tell you all of my dirty little secrets, although I doubt your mother would approve." Echo's voice dripped with sarcasm.

What the hell, maybe it's time I got this off of my chest. Then she was struck with a brilliant notion; sex talk can lead to sex acts. Since their passionate kiss in the kitchen, Flynn had been the picture of gentlemanly behavior. Perhaps some scintillating conversation would change that.

"Alright, I'll tell you, but I'm warning you, it is deliciously depraved."

"Mmmm," Flynn responded rubbing his palms together. "I can hardly wait."

"Here's goes." Echo took a deep breath.

"Okay, I fantasize that I am being dominated by someone. I don't mean someone who abuses me, because that is not cool at all." She shook her head, screwing up her face in displeasure. "I would have to trust them. That's an important prerequisite. I do have my boundaries," she clarified.

She checked Flynn's face for a negative emotion, but found only a hint of a smile. *He might actually be enjoying this! Was it turning him on?* Just thinking about being dominated was turning her on. She needed to feel the reassurance of his body next to hers as she immersed herself in the details of her fantasy.

Snuggling her head against Flynn's chest, she closed her eyes, envisioning the details of her fantasy, and the words tumbled from her mouth. "It goes something like this; my partner knows that it excites me when he takes control, and I am a little frightened…not of him, just of not knowing what is going to happen…and that makes it all the more exciting. He tells me what to do and how to do it, and then he *makes* me do it. All the while, everything he commands is aimed at giving me pleasure, even if it doesn't at first appear like that.

Because I trust him, he is able to get me to try all sorts of exotic things I've never experienced before, and I love it. I do *everything* he wants me to do. I allow him to dominate the hell out of me and it drives me wild with passion. He is white-hot with desire when I submit to him, but he stops short of screwing me to the bedpost until he has me moaning and writhing, begging for it. I offer my body to him to do with as he wishes and he teases and taunts me, controlling my response until he gives me permission for release.

We go beyond the usual sexual experience into something more exciting, more fulfilling, more… dangerous! It's an entire erotic lifestyle that goes past the bedroom door and spills into my daily life. Just imagine any day of your life, and then imagine the same day, but every minute of it has this underlying sexual tension that builds and builds until finally we…I mean, me and my lover unleash it."

Echo braced for Flynn's reaction. "There you have it. You think I'm freak, don't you?"

Flynn coughed nervously, his cheeks flushing a rosy red. "Not at all,

I find it quite, um, stimulating…and I can prove it. Look at my wanker."
Flynn leaned back against the couch revealing a substantial swelling
in his trousers.

Bleary eyed, Echo focused on the bulging fabric of Flynn's crotch.
Good Lord, this man was packing heat. A wide hillock extended from
between his legs, traversing upward towards his belt buckle. Its girth
pushed the waistband of his pants away from his skin. Like a Moray eel
emerging from the seafloor, it snaked towards his navel, the swollen head
trapped between his trousers and the coarse black hairs of his abdomen.
I knew it! I just knew he had a giant-sized jackhammer! Echo was impressed,
and flattered. A shiver ran through her body when she considered the
pummeling promise of what lay beneath his pants. She leaned into him,
drunkenly punctuating her words by poking Flynn in the chest with
her finger. "That…my friend…should require you…to carry a license."

Flynn shifted in his seat. "I'm glad that you approve." He adjusted
his pants to conceal his enlarging prick and nervously cleared his throat.
"So back to this fantasy of yours, have you thought about playing it out
for real?"

Echo had indeed thought about it. It was on her top-five list of things
she wanted to do, right beneath winning the lottery and partying with
Jack Nicholson.

"Oh that…sure, I've thought about it, but I don't really see myself
ever being in the right…*hic*…Excuse me…circumstances for it to happen.
Plus, I think I might be too big a chicken."

"But what if everything was right? The right person, the right
circumstances? Do you think you would give it a go?"

"I don't know. What are you suggheshting?" Echo slurred. Damn,
slurring her words was her personal red flag that she was past the point
of no return.

"Nothing, just asking."

An awkward silence ensued. Echo wondered where he was going
with this line of questioning. Her head swam from too much wine and
the need for sleep nagged at her eyelids. Leaning against the back of
the sofa, she closed her eyes.

After a protracted moment, Flynn patted Echo's knee. "I better get
you to bed and call it a night."

Flynn lifted Echo's slackened form into his capable arms. A blissful
state of drowsiness descended upon her body. Luxuriating in the

sensation, she nestled her face into his muscled neck and filled her lungs with his intoxicating scent.

While Echo basked in his manly essence, Flynn ascended the stairs which led to her bedroom, then deposited her on the bed.

Echo watched him through one drowsy eye. She considered it entirely possible that he was even sexier when she was drunk.

"Where are your nightclothes?" Flynn whispered into her ear.

His breath tickled, causing lovely little shivers to spiral down her spine. Echo nestled her face deeply into the cool comfort of the pillow and mumbled, "Don't have any...I sleep in the nuuuude."

The woolly weight of a blanket parachuted onto her body. Flynn's hands slid beneath her back as he tucked it around her. Echo was about to lift the blanket and invite him inside of her cozy cocoon when she heard him say, "Okay darlin', I'm just going to go now."

Flynn began to tiptoe towards the door. "Thanks for a terrific evening. It was grand, really it was."

What! He was leaving just like that? Without as much as a kiss?

Enough of this gentlemanly act. Talking about her fantasy had made her horny as a high-school senior and she wanted to fall asleep with the taste of his tongue in her mouth.

Echo was fully alert now. She may have been drunk but she wasn't stupid. She batted her lashes and engaged her most pathetic puppy-dog expression. "Flynn, aren't you going to kiss me goodnight?"

Flynn halted mid-step.

"Oh, how terrible of me to forget." He said. "No tucking-in is complete without the required goodnight kiss."

Echo tried to hide the hint of a smile that pulled on the corners of her mouth. Her little scheme had worked. Flynn approached. Tilting her face towards his, she licked her lips, parting them slightly, and waited for his kiss.

Bending low, Flynn placed a peck on Echo's forehead, followed by a disappointing pat on the top of her head.

Echo's body squirmed from the frustration that was building inside of her. Dammit, here she was offering herself to him and he seemed impervious to her charms. Now he was just fucking with her—and maybe making fun of her a little bit too. Not nice. She was determined to have the last word. There was not a chance in hell she was going to allow him to scoot out of her bedroom like this. Before he left tonight, she wanted to give him something to think about…maybe even something to go home and jerk off to. Yeah, give him a little hint of what he was missing.

"Not from way up there," Echo pouted, thumping the mattress with her palm. "Sit here. I want a proper kiss."

Echo's game was transparent and Flynn determined to give her a taste of her own medicine. Conjuring his best predatory countenance, he leered unblinkingly into her eyes. She leered back, with an expression of victory on her face.

Flynn pounced onto the bed, capturing her hips between his knees. A startled gasp escaped from Echo's throat. Flynn stroked her hair, which fanned out across the pillow like the coral rays of a sunset. She arched her neck, turning her face upward and closed her eyes.

Flynn knew that he could have her tonight if he chose to. He would have liked nothing more than to tumble between the sheets with this lovely lass. She was the epitome of what he desired; flowing red hair, translucent skin, spectacular breasts, all wrapped in one lusty package. But tonight was too soon. He wanted to be more than a brief encounter to her, another notch on her bedpost. She might fuck him, but he wanted to make certain that she would never forget him.

Entwining a fistful of Echo's hair in his fingers he tugged it sharply backward. The startled look on Echo's face was priceless. At first she was wide-eyed with shock, but her expression quickly melted into electrified anticipation. Her nostrils flared and a fire burned hotly in her eyes. Flynn knew he had struck a chord in her. The rapid rise and fall of her breasts as her breathing quickened also struck a chord in him and he felt a stir at the base of his prick. Dominating her in this way was unexpectedly arousing. Masculinity seemed to surge through every cell of his body.

Like a panther stalking its prey, he inched nearer to her waiting mouth until he could feel her breath on his skin. She lay in motionless anticipation, narrowing her gaze and daring him to take the lead. In a flash his mouth descended on hers. His probing tongue invaded her lips. Echo squirmed beneath his body, her breasts pressing against his chest, her hips writhing on the mattress.

She stretched her arms to embrace his neck, but Flynn quickly clutched her wrists pinning them to the headboard.

The act of restraining her arms seemed to embolden her.

She played with his tongue as if she was pleasuring his prick. Sucking it in and out her mouth, she swirled her tongue along the length of his, taking it deeply into her throat. He responded, sinking his tongue into her, and imagining his cock filling her mouth as he wrestled this wildcat woman into submission.

Thrusting her hips upward, she ground her loins against his enlarging cock. She wasn't shy about her desire. A hot-blooded woman was to his liking, but a hot-blooded woman that was begging to be tamed was damn near irresistible. The most shocking thoughts ran through his mind: Echo on her knees, his cock teasing her mouth, Echo in restraints, helpless as his tongue explored every inch of her flesh, and Echo wailing for him to fuck her. If he wasn't careful, he could easily be swept up in this new found power.

The blanket that had covered her was now bunched up to one side.

Flynn pulled his mouth from hers, his eyes roaming the landscape of her form. The round buds of her nipples jutted against her shirt; her flesh glowed with a lusty, rosy hue. Her skirt was hiked up over her hips, revealing the curving mound of her pussy beneath her barely-there panties. On the comforter beneath her hips, spread a wide circle of wet desire.

His cock urged him to take it to the finish, but his better judgment won out. If he allowed himself in her bed, he would be giving her what she craved—he would be handing himself over to her on a silver platter too easily. If he lay with her tonight, he might never want to leave. Abruptly, he released her wrists, and leapt to his feet. Echo stared at him, breathless.

"I think that should hold you for a while," he said, pretending a composure he didn't feel. He had to get out of her bedroom before he took things too far.

Flynn crossed to the door. Just before pulling it shut behind him, he paused long enough to call out over his shoulder, "Sleep tight, and be careful what *you* wish for, Miss Sullivan."

A Proposition

Flynn and Echo became fast friends. He helped her get acquainted with her new surroundings. They took leisurely strolls through the neighborhood, cuddled on the sofa, went antiquing; that was Flynn's idea, and bickered at least twice a day. In short, they were falling in love.

More and more Echo dared to think about the possibility that this might be "the one." But other than snuggling and extended soulful kisses, Flynn had made no further moves of a sexual nature, which Echo found frustrating as hell. She began to doubt her own powers of feminine persuasion. Day and night she fantasized about him. The maddening memory of his demonstration of domination made her heart race and her hand reach instinctively to caress her lonely pussy.

One evening, over an especially tasty meal that Echo had prepared, Flynn offered up a proposition.

"Echo, I've been doing some thinking." Flynn seemed uncharacteristically nervous. In fact, all day Echo had noticed that his demeanor had been a bit off. He had been distant and preoccupied.

She braced herself for a letdown. *If a man says they have been doing some thinking, it can only mean one thing; he's breaking up with me.*

Echo stopped chewing her food. She had suddenly lost her appetite.

She fortified her courage by draining the last drop of wine from her glass, and steeled herself for the "let's just be friends" speech. "You know that…um…fantasy of yours?" Flynn began, nervously clearing his throat.

There it was. She had run him off with her erotic imaginings. He had probably been thinking about it ever since that drunken night, and now just couldn't bring himself to get involved with a woman he considered to be a deviant. How unfair. He had promised!

"You swore that you wouldn't hold it against me."

Flynn reached across the table. Cradling her hand in both of his, he offered reassurance. "Believe me; I am not holding it against you. I was just wondering, did you really mean what you said?"

Echo squirmed in her chair. Did she really mean it? It certainly was her favorite and most reliable fantasy. It was the one that she turned to again and again, and it never disappointed. She wondered what answer Flynn was hoping to hear. Was he into it…or not? She reflected again on the memory of their heated encounter in her bed. She knew that he had sort of played with the notion then, and she had certainly and most decidedly enjoyed it, but was it a role that turned him on, or had it only been the alcohol talking?

If he didn't like what he heard, this could be the beginning of the end. She truly did have a yearning to explore this side of her sexuality, but if it meant losing him, she would be willing to push it aside for now… if she could.

The memory of that one night, him looming over her, pulling roughly on her hair, and his hands imprisoning her wrists, made her breathless. If they were to become sexual with each other, it wouldn't be long before she would beg him to dominate her for real.

Echo stared down at their hands, her fingers lightly playing through his. She couldn't look into his eyes. Her cheeks grew warm as a blush of embarrassment blossomed on her face.

"Gosh honestly, I don't know if I meant it or not. So far it's just been a fantasy, and fantasies are safe. I do know that I am very intrigued by it. That night, on my bed…when you sort of …you know…that was just the sexiest, most exciting thing to me.

I don't know why I feel this way. I think it's because most of the time I'm the take charge type and it would be really freeing to give that up for a few hours and have some fun. Plus, I just don't stay interested in men that I can walk all over. Where's the challenge in that? I suppose I have this vision of a strong, domineering man who isn't intimidated by me. I've never deliberately sought out that type of relationship, but I suppose that if the right person came along, I would be open to it."

"Echo," Flynn locked his eyes on hers. "I'm trying to say…if you're hiring, I'd like to apply for the position."

This unexpected proposition stunned Echo to the core. He was serious! She had braced herself for the opposite reaction…had practically had her "but I'd forget it all, if you want me to" speech ready to go in case she needed it. She really wasn't expecting this.

She pulled her hand from his, sitting back in her chair. Her heart was pounding inside of her chest and she wondered if Flynn could detect it fluttering against the thin fabric of her blouse. Perspiration crept from under her arms and she held them tightly against her body. She was dizzy with questions. It had always been just a fantasy for her, and Flynn was proposing that she take the next great leap into some erotic unknown. She needed clarification.

"What exactly do you mean?" she asked.

"I know this seems sudden, but I have given this a great deal of thought. I didn't want to broach the subject with you until I was certain, but when something is right, it's right. You don't have to fantasize about what you want when it's standing right in front of you. I want to take our relationship to the next level and if you'll have me, I would like you to consider me for the role of your Master."

Master…the word sounded strange. Would that make her his slave? And on what terms…for a few hours, a few days… in the bedroom, out of the bedroom? She hadn't truly considered all of the possibilities and complications until now.

She had always imagined that her fantasy would somehow just happen, that she would simply find herself swept up in the powerful lure of a hypnotic dominant who would swoop down on her helpless, but willing body like a mesmerizing vampire upon his victim. But Flynn was making a formal proposition about something that she wasn't certain she had a complete understanding of.

The offer was enticing. She had wanted a sexual relationship with Flynn almost from the first moment they had met. In fact, she had thought of little else. Now he was proposing something that seemed much more intimate than casual coupling. She wondered if he even knew what he was asking.

"Flynn, I have to ask…have you done this sort of thing before?"

Flynn sipped from his wine glass. "Let's just say that I am familiar with what's expected of me. Since you asked, I was wondering what you knew about the lifestyle."

Intrigued by the lifestyle, Echo had once gotten up the nerve to go to a fetish ball where she was captivated by the myriad expressions of sexuality. Drawn to the couples that expressed a submissive/dominant relationship, she studied their actions with fascination, seeing a touching beauty in them. Afterwards, Echo researched the psychology of a submissive, and it was as if they had read her diary. Since then, she had delved into books and movies depicting submissives. Each story was different, some extreme and some much tamer, but through them she had learned and been able to explore what she found exciting and what she didn't.

"I think I know enough to not be shocked about certain aspects of it." She explained. "I guess I'm not certain if I know what I should."

"That part you can leave up to me. It would be my responsibility to instruct and nurture you along the way. You need to have confidence in me and I need to make certain that your confidence is well placed.

Don't kid yourself that it will be easy, and I may not always be exactly what you want, but I sure as hell will try my damnedest to please you. I promise to always keep your best interest at heart and not to progress faster than you're ready. If you believe in me, I can give you what you don't yet know that you need."

Echo's stomach tightened at his words. Where had she heard that before? She couldn't quite recall. More frequently than coincidence could explain, Flynn would say things that Echo was certain she'd heard before. It was happening once more…déjà vu, all over again.

Echo carefully weighed Flynn's words, searching for a trace of insincerity. Did she trust him? She had issues with trust regarding any man, but she did trust Flynn. He had been nothing but honorable since they met. Still she hesitated, fearful to leap into the unknown. She chewed her bottom lip in indecision.

Flynn's voice took on a sense of urgency. "Take a chance on me, Echo. It's a gamble, I know. I'm not perfect, and there are certain aspects of my personality that I know I will have to work on, but I'll try my best to be what you want me to be.

It's completely your choice," he persisted. "But I need you to know that I want this too. I could hardly believe my good luck when you expressed your feelings to me the other night. Then, when I was on your bed, and playing around with being dominant, something clicked. We seem so right together that it's almost spooky."

It *was* spooky. Fate was not something she readily believed in, but all the signs pointed to this moment. She realized her biggest fear was that she would somehow fuck this up and lose him.

"What happens," she asked, "if I find I can't do it, or don't like it?"

"If it doesn't work out, there will be no hard feelings, and hopefully we remain good friends, perhaps even more. I should have said this sooner, in case you couldn't tell, but I really care for you, lass and if you say yes, I promise you that I will cherish your submission as the most precious gift I have ever received, and in turn I will do my damnedest to take your mind and body to places that you have never even imagined."

No one had ever promised to take her mind and body to unimagined places. If she could choose anyone to do that to her, it would definitely be Flynn. He had already taken her mind on flights of fancy. He had been the leading character in her solo sexual acts since day one, and she hadn't been able to bump him from the starring role since. She yearned to be with him in the flesh. In the back of her mind, she suspected that having sex with him could be the wildest, most erotic experience of her life and she was compelled to find out if her suspicions were true.

"You know what Flynn—yes, I say yes, let's do it."

He couldn't believe his own ears. Relief, mingled with a sense of excitement tingled beneath his skin. Flynn's thoughts were abuzz as he leaned back against the chair, nearly toppling it to the floor. His joy quickly turned sober as the serious nature of his business descended upon his mind. The confidence he had felt during his conversation with Echo waned. He had one chance to get this right. The slightest error and she would be lost to him. It was not only her body she had entrusted to him, but her heart and her psyche were now in his care as well.

Throughout his life he had fearlessly gone to battle for his land, encountered countless foes, and faced demons of every sort, but none intimidated him more than this one mortal woman.

A Lesson in Submission

The morning broke dazzling and clear. The earth announced the arrival of changing seasons with the clean snap of a crisp October chill. Coffee cup in hand, Echo padded out to the mailbox, her fuzzy terry slippers flap flapping on the sidewalk.

Utility bills, a credit card offer, coupons, she thought as she flipped through the mail. *Ooh, what's this?* She turned the small white envelope over in her hands. A wax impression of a mask sealed the flap. Echo didn't wait until she was back in the house to open the intriguing correspondence. Carefully lifting the wax seal, she sat on her porch and opened the letter. A single piece of cardstock was enclosed.

'You are cordially invited to explore your innermost desires at a Halloween Fantasy Ball, 8 pm, October 31st. Dress accordingly, Flynn.'

Echo gathered up her mail and darted inside of the house. She examined the envelope. It bore no return address or postage mark. Flynn must have snuck over and tucked it into her mailbox while she was sleeping. Echo read the invitation once more.

Dress accordingly? What in the heck does that mean?

"You can decide to be whatever you want to be…so decide who you truly want to be?"

Echo reeled around expecting to see Flynn. The door was shut tightly behind her. She was alone in the house. The words floated like a specter in the shadows.

Echo had the sneaking suspicion that someone in the great beyond was having some fun with her by impersonating Flynn's voice.

"Well for your information, that is exactly what I am going to do!" she declared to no one in particular.

* * *

Echo's exhilaration mounted as she peered into the window of the costume shop. Halloween was her favorite time of year. She reveled in the comically ghastly images, the sinister, grinning Jack-O-Lanterns, and all things that go bump in the night. What she most anticipated were the few fantastical hours when she could become whoever she wanted to be. As she donned each element of her chosen costume a gradual transformation would come over her personality. With the final stroke of makeup, she was not Echo any longer. She was Cinderella at the ball, racing to outrun the stroke of midnight that announced her return to reality.

A bell tinkled merrily over the door as she entered the crowded store. The shop was a Halloween enthusiast's dream. Gruesome props, peculiar masks and hundreds of costume choices lined the walls.

"Where to begin...?" Echo considered. "Hmm, this is pretty." She placed a pink sequined mask over her eyes.

"No, not that one. Let's try...this."

Echo froze. Was someone standing behind her, or was it an unearthly trickster again? Nowadays she couldn't trust her own judgment. Echo inhaled sharply as the pretty pink mask was pulled from her face and swiftly replaced with another. Who was touching her? She tried to turn around, but unseen hands gripped her firmly by the shoulders and faced her towards a mirror. She was thrilled and relieved to see Flynn's rugged face in the reflection. Echo chided herself for being so jumpy. Flynn probably thought she was a basket case. How could he know that disembodied voices followed her around?

Resting his chin on the top of her head, he purred, "Now, doesn't this mask suit you better?"

Echo studied her reflection. The upper half of her face was obscured by a mask of white leather that was so thin and supple it felt as if a fine kid glove embraced her skin. Her emerald eyes peered out from beneath the silvery eyebrows embossed on the mask. She was speechless, transfixed upon her reflection.

"Your silence tells me that you approve. Now we have to select your costume. You *are* here buying a costume for my party?"

She beamed a smile. "You bet I am. I love costume parties!"

"Well, let's see. How fun. You can be anyone you want to be...so, you need to decide who you truly want to be."

Okay, this was just too weird. She had heard those words just this morning. Now she was certain someone was playing tricks on her.

"I guess that's the problem," she chuckled. "I don't really know who

I want to be."

"Alright, then, see that clerk over there?" Flynn lowered his voice to a conspiratorial whisper. "Go over to him and tell him that you would like to try on something that accents your assets, and flash him that same smile you just gave me."

Echo shot Flynn a questioning look. She began to suspect that he was up to something.

"Go on, be a good girl." Flynn prodded her forward with a slight push against her back.

"I'm going…I'm going." Echo proceeded hesitantly towards the clerk when a sharp snap stung her buttocks. Turning in surprise, she saw Flynn, grinning slyly, and twirling a riding crop in his hand.

"Giddy up little filly, we don't have all day!"

Echo's ass cheek burned from the crop. She knew that she should be put off by his audacious behavior, but she wasn't. In fact, her body pulsed with stimulation in response to Flynn's bold advances.

She leaned over the glass counter, her breasts resting on her folded arms causing her cleavage to deepen and swell above the scooped neckline of her tank top. She spied Flynn from the corner of her eye and purposefully swayed her bottom to and fro as she flirted shamelessly with the man behind the counter. An unhappy expression crossed Flynn's face. He was obviously the jealous type. Echo relished having the power to evoke those feelings from him.

The acne-scarred clerk leered lasciviously as he guided Echo to a room that was obscured by a heavy black curtain. Sizing her up, he selected an ivory leather fishtail gown and displayed it for her inspection. The decadent gown sported a daringly low-cut corseted bustier. A wide silver zipper ran from just below the knees to slightly above the navel. The dress was fully boned, lacing from top to bottom in the back. The costume was clearly designed to scandalously expose the wearer's ass no matter how tightly the laces were cinched.

"That one's open," instructed the clerk, pointing to a dressing room.

"Do you need any assistance getting into that little number, because I could probably leave the floor for a few minutes?"

"No, thank you," Echo demurred. "I think I can manage." Echo pushed the dressing room door open. From inside the cubicle a hand reached out, snatched her by the wrist and jerked her inside. Echo's heart pounded in alarm. Another hand clamped over her mouth. "Don't scream." Flynn's eyes sparkled back at her in the full length mirror. "Jesus Christ, you scared the crap out of me!" she hissed. "But that's half the fun," he whispered. "And I couldn't live another minute without doing *this*." Flynn's arms encircled her waist, pulling her to him. She adored the warmth of his body against her skin. She combed her fingers through his dark hair, loving the softness of the silky strands as she wound them around her fingertips.

His mouth met hers in a tender kiss. She parted her lips to receive his tongue. The taste of warm peppermint tingled on her taste buds. His tongue tickled the roof of her mouth. As if on cue, her body answered with a rush of dampness between her legs.

"What are you doing to me?" she murmured.

Placing his mouth on her ear, Flynn soothed, "You are dreaming and you don't even know that you are asleep."

It was happening again. The words that had been following her around were coming out of Flynn's mouth. Echo's thoughts raced. Try as she might, she couldn't think of an explanation.

In her excitement over seeing Flynn, she hadn't stopped to consider how it happened that she had just run into him in the shop. Her woman's intuition told her that it was more than a happy coincidence.

"Flynn, I'm ecstatic to see you, but what, exactly, are you doing here?"

"Well, lass, school is in session and lesson number one has already begun." Placing the tip of the riding crop on the neckline of her baby blue tank top, he commanded, "Remove it...slowly."

"What? Here? Flynn, you have to be joking?"

"No joke, it's for real this time. Are you going to do what I tell you or should we call the whole thing off?"

Flynn had never been so boldly forthright with her. Echo's body sizzled with excitement when he spoke to her in that way. She could tell by the look in his eye, something naughty was on his mind.

"Alright," she agreed. "But what do you have planned?"

"That, my dear," taunted Flynn, "is for me to know and for you to find out. Now, remove that sexy little top and let me see what we're working with."

Well, he wanted to see what she was working with, did he? A little semi-private striptease is what he was requesting. *I can handle that*, Echo decided. *Let's see if he can.*

Echo pulled the blue tank top out of her jeans. Gathering the hem in her hands she suggestively wiggled the fabric above her waistline. At a snail's pace she revealed her body to Flynn. She paused for a moment when her blushing nipples, protruding from puckered areolas, popped into view. She allowed Flynn one enticing moment to survey her tightening nubs before lifting the top over her head and tossing it into the corner. Her magnificent, plump breasts were less than an inch from Flynn's face as he sat on the bench in the cramped dressing room. The clattering of hangers resounded from the adjoining changing room.

Flynn spoke in a low voice, "I want a taste."

I'll bet you do. Echo leaned towards Flynn, touching a nipple to his mouth. Her stomach tightened as the tip of his tongue fluttered over the tingling bud. She teased him, brushing her nipples across his lips. This was the first time in many months that she had felt the intimate touch of another person. Her body eagerly responded when Flynn parted his lips, and then alternately grasped the nipples between his teeth, tugging them. The stimulation of her hyper-sensitive breasts awakened her slumbering libido. What before had been a dewy dampness between her legs was now a raging river spilling over its swollen banks.

As he wetted and teased her tender nipples, she detected the feather-light touch of the crop as Flynn dragged it upward along her inner thigh, inching it ever northward towards the damp ringlet that was forming on her jeans. When he twitched the crop handle, snapping a stinging rap to Echo's pussy, she found the punishing vibration thrilling. Sweeping the crop against the thick center seam of her pants, Flynn fluttered the tip from back to front. The lightness of the touch tickled Echo in all the right places. Flynn brought the small whip to rest on the zipper of her pants. Another twitch and the crop snapped once more. Flynn wanted her out of her jeans, and she was happy to oblige. She liked this new adventure. She was being bad, and it felt decadently good.

Echo eased her jeans off of her hips, revealing her red panties. The jeans dropped to the floor. Stepping clear of the bunched denim, she kicked them under the bench with the toe of her pumps.

She studied Flynn's face for a reaction. She knew that she was striking. She hoped he thought so too. Flynn's response was so dramatic that it took her by surprise. Flynn dropped to his knees and pushed her legs apart. Placing his hands around her buttocks, he inhaled her musk through the lace of her panties. His whiskers broke through the thin fabric and prickled the skin of her pudendum.

Echo rejoiced. Flynn was on his knees with his face buried in her pussy as if she had just presented him with a priceless gift.

"You are more exquisite than I've imagined." He choked.

Her pride swelled. Any inhibitions that she still clung to dropped away in the face of the power of her femininity. She moaned, pressing Flynn's mouth onto her pussy, delighting in the warmth of his lips on hers. "Now, be very still, very quiet," he admonished as he pulled his mouth from her. Echo quieted her moaning and made a conscious effort to slow her breathing. As she silenced her body, she became aware of the noises outside of the dressing room. The ring of the cash register, the ting-a-ling of the bell over the doorway, and the conversations that drifted in and out of earshot, made her realize that they, too, might be overheard. It was dangerous and thrilling.

Flynn reached over to the door, turning the lock. Hooking his fingers inside the thin straps of her thong, Flynn inched the small bit of lace down the length of Echo's legs. Her lubrication had soaked so thoroughly into the thin fabric that it was as if she was stepping out of a wet bathing suit bottom. The subtle aroma of her musk reached her nostrils.

Flynn rocked back on his heels to free her feet from the panties, and Echo saw that his cock was full and straining beneath the confines of his trousers. If she could only touch him, what would he feel like in her hands? She imagined his tool would be so thick and rigid that she could barely wrap her fingers around it.

She rubbed the toe of her shoe against his turgid member. Flynn bit his lip and groaned. She saw a look of exquisite torture on his face and she understood exactly what he was feeling. She felt the same. She wanted to surrender herself to him—to have his hands and mouth ravishing every inch of her flesh. The only thing holding her back from tearing the clothing from his body was her rapidly wavering self-control.

Flynn placed her foot back on the floor.

"Put your hands on my shoulders. Remember," he admonished, "not a solitary sound from you."

Echo braced her weight on Flynn's shoulders, and steadied her shuddering limbs. The feathery caress of his fingers tickled the sensitive skin on her inner thighs as they skimmed their way upward towards her heat. Echo's flesh twitched and prickled as his fingers crawled over her body. From her vantage point, she had a view of his thick, glossy black curls. She longed to wrap her arms around his head and immerse her face in his hair.

Flynn put his lips to her pussy. The warmth of his mouth penetrated the steamy wetness of her sex. Echo's breath caught in her throat and she had to remind herself to exhale. The breath left her lungs in small, shuddering gasps.

She rose up on her toes when his enthusiastic tongue skillfully parted her lips and entered her. It swirled around inside of her, lapping the slippery cream that coated the walls of her cock canal.

Had anyone ever died from too much pleasure? A whirring sound droned in her head, blocking out everything but the ecstasy between her legs, as Flynn's touch transported her to a wakeful state of bliss. Echo closed her eyes, and dropped her head backwards, submitting to his feverish touch.

A gentle tugging vibration engulfed her clitoris as Flynn lured it between his lips, fluttering his tongue over and around the undulating jewel. Her knees weakened. She gripped Flynn's shoulders, her hips rocking instinctively. Flynn's fingernails pressed sharply into her buttocks, pressing her pussy to his mouth. He suckled her clit, coaxing the relentless craving ever closer to the surface. The first tingling of impending orgasm twitched through her veins.

Echo's blood pulsed beneath her skin. Her hands jumped involuntarily against his shoulders.

Flynn eased his mouth from her sex. The sound of his whisper broke through the wall of rapture that had surrounded her senses. "Turn around, face the mirror, and place your hands on the wall," he instructed.

He was going to fuck her from behind, Echo was certain of it. Right here in this claustrophobic dressing room, while the world passed so near to them, he was going to bang her against the thin walls and he wanted her to watch it happen in the mirror's reflection. She wanted to look in his eyes when he first penetrated her. She wanted to see what his face looked like when he climaxed.

Echo placed both hands flat against the wall. Her reflection showed a tell-tale red flush over her breasts and face.

Flynn remained kneeling on the floor. He pulled her hips towards him, arching her back in an exaggerated pose. Echo readied herself to receive his cock, but instead she experienced the sensation of tiny bites on her behind. She looked in the mirror to see Flynn nibbling her ass.

The little bites didn't really hurt, but they awakened a strange yearning in her. She wanted to feel his teeth penetrate more sharply into her skin. She craved to walk the knife's edge of pain and pleasure. When the pressure from his teeth dented her flesh, she moaned with delight and pushed her ass more firmly against his mouth.

Flynn pressed his palms against Echo's buttocks, spreading her cheeks and exposing her small dark hole. His tongue was fiercely hot against her tender flesh as it swirled around the tight opening. Fearing that she might cry out, Echo clamped her jaw, gritting her teeth. A finger, maybe two, she couldn't tell, eased their way into the shadowy hole, bringing with them an exquisite, burning bliss.

Echo's palms slid down the wall. She struggled to regain her balance.

The clamor of the busy shop outside intruded into her ears. She had almost forgotten where she was. She tried to calculate how long she and Flynn had been locked in the dressing room. It could have been minutes, or hours, she couldn't tell. The sound of footsteps passing very near the door thrilled her. Knowing that she was having this secret moment in such a public place heightened her arousal. Her breasts tingled with heaviness, and she thrust her hips towards Flynn, begging him to fill her. A cool, firm object penetrated her pussy. In the reflection, Echo saw Flynn stroking and twirling the riding crop inside of her. It blew her mind.

It was so kinky, but so decadently erotic. The sleek, rigid crop tickled secret places inside of her that a penis couldn't. Echo rode unabashedly on the phallic invader, her juices coursing down the inside of her legs.

She bucked her hips. Her legs trembled as her hands pressed firmly against the wall. She caught Flynn's eye in the mirror and saw her own eyes, wide with pleasured torment.

"It's okay, baby," Flynn soothed, "let it out. Show me what you've got." The sound of Flynn's voice was the impetus that she needed to take her over the edge. She bore down, squeezing the object penetrating her pussy and grinding against Flynn's fingers. Every muscle in her body, down to the tiniest ones, began to tremor. A roar resounded in Echo's head. Her panting breaths abruptly halted as the muscles in her neck tensed. She threw her head back, all of her senses focused on her orgasm. Like the pounding surf, it washed over her, engulfing everything in its path, then gradually retreated, depositing her lightheaded and listless upon the shore.

Flynn held her tightly around the waist, his hand pressed against her throbbing clitoris until the spasms subsided. Exhausted, Echo's ankles gave out and she stumbled against the wall.

"Are you alright?" Flynn asked.

Echo gulped and nodded her head.

"You were wonderful, you know…just perfect." Flynn was kissing her flesh, but her body, numbed from the electricity of her orgasm, barely felt his lips. "Now let's get you dressed, girl. I want you to leave the costume and mask with the clerk and tell him that you've changed your mind."

Reality was crawling its way back into Echo's consciousness. She felt so strange, as if she had viewed her actions from a far-off perspective. It was as if she had experienced sexual stimulation for the very first time.

She had never been that unguarded. Flynn had somehow released a part of her that was entirely new. She wanted to say something to Flynn, but she didn't even know exactly what.

"Flynn, I…"

"Shhh," he placed a finger to her lips. "No words."

Mutely, Flynn dressed Echo in her familiar jeans and tank. She went through the motions in a daze.

Echo slipped out the door of the dressing room and back into the busy shop. She performed as she had been instructed, handing the costume pieces back to the disinterested clerk. As she was leaving the store, the sound of Flynn's voice reached her ears over the clamor of the busy shop.

"I've decided that I won't need this after all."

Glancing backward, she saw Flynn smiling broadly as he slapped the riding crop into the hands of the cashier.

Echo's face blushed a deep crimson. *Oh no, he didn't!* She thought, shaking her head in disbelief.

The Green Eyed Monster

Echo gazed out of her kitchen window at the back garden, which had turned from shades of pink and blue to the golden hues of autumn. She was a churning mass of emotions. She felt like Alice in Wonderland tumbling ass over teacups down the rabbit hole. The genie was out of the bottle and there was no sending him back. With eager anticipation, she looked forward to her next encounter with Flynn…Flynn, who in the wink of an eye had changed everything.

Her response to him had been dramatic. What kind of hold did he possess on her? From the moment he entered her life, he was perpetually in her thoughts. A single fleeting image of him caused her to feel fragile and dreamy.

It was more than lust. He had stirred up emotions that she had long ago locked away. She was vulnerable, and it was this vulnerability that frightened her. It was one thing to give control over to him for sexual games, but quite another to give her heart to him. Was he just someone to roll around in bed with and share a few laughs, or was he the answer to her prayers?

Her mother had told her that she would know when the right man came along. But her mother believed in things like fate and destiny. Echo was far more practical. Still, she wished that she had a way to contact her mother.

* * *

Inside the soaring turret room, encircled by towering windows, Flynn slumped in an oversize leather chair. One leg stretched out in front of him, the other bent and nervously fidgeting. His hands pressed together forming a steeple, his index fingers like a metronome, tapping out his troubled thoughts.

Something wasn't right. She was too willing, too eager. It was too easy. Flynn rolled the possibilities over in his mind.

His powers of persuasion were first-rate, perhaps too effective. She had seemed entirely sincere, but then again, so far it had been all fun and games. For what lay ahead, she would have to trust him with her very life. Today was a good beginning and a gateway into earning that trust. Flynn commended himself for choosing a public place for their first encounter. Despite the danger of being discovered, it actually was a safe haven for her, a place so full of people that she knew he couldn't do anything to her without consent. Not that he would have.

In just a few weeks she would have to be fully ready, completely and without reservation invested in their relationship, and wholly confident of him. She had not truly been put to the test yet. Progress had been made, but Flynn didn't fool himself into thinking that the road was paved before him. Echo was high-spirited and strong-willed. There would be bumps along the way.

In the background a mantle clock ticked off the minutes, reminding Flynn that there was no time to waste, and no room for error. He had to step on the accelerator and push things forward. He pressed his fingers to his lips. They still bore the scent of her. Inhaling her musk into his lungs, his impatient prick stirred. Flynn laughed out loud at the irony. She was the submissive, yet he was the one being punished.

"Patience, ole chap," Flynn admonished his pecker. "You'll get your chance soon enough."

Flynn knew he mustn't allow his desire for her to cloud his thinking. He was already struggling with the difficult task of bringing her face to face with her destiny. He found it almost impossible to be a stern Master with her. He only wanted to please her, to make her happy; however that wasn't what this was about. The sexual game was merely a doorway, a shortcut.

He was the one that had recognized her as the fulfillment of the prophecy. He was the one that pleaded with the Counsel to do this thing. Now it was solely in his hands to complete the mission. If he could slowly and subtly instruct her to follow his lead when she was at her most vulnerable, she would be trained and conditioned to willingly surrender to him when he asked for her life.

He pondered the possibility that he was misreading the situation. Perhaps things were exactly as they appeared. Perhaps she was as ready as her response indicated. Yet Flynn knew enough not to fool himself into believing that he had Echo in the palm of his hand. In truth, he was more concerned that *he* was the one with his heart strung on the line. If events didn't go as planned, he was certain to be a doomed man.

From his vantage point in the turret, Flynn spied a cable company van pull up to the curb outside of her house. A sandy-haired man hopped out, his wide tool belt jangling as his feet met the pavement.

Flynn sprinted to the window and tracked the man's movements as he swaggered up the sidewalk towards Echo's door, finally disappearing behind a large elm.

Flynn paced and waited. An hour passed, then two.

What the hell is going on in there? Flynn's blood began to simmer. *Two hours to lay some bloody cable! Cable had better be the only thing that bastard is laying!*

Flynn didn't plan on contacting Echo again so soon after her first lesson, but this cable fellow was really getting on his nerves.

It's past five o'clock. What is this cheeky jack-off doing working past five?

Flynn's active imagination took a dark turn. He envisioned the man's hands on Echo's body, his tongue thrust into her mouth, his cock inside of her.

"That's it!" Flynn declared. "I am bloody well going over there!"

* * *

With purposeful strides, Flynn marched up the sidewalk.

"Knock, knock," he bellowed, booting the unlatched door open.

He stomped into the living room. An advertisement for Pop-it Toaster Treats blared from the television, but there was no sign of Echo or the cable man. Flynn made a sweep of the first floor rooms; all vacant as well.

Echo's infectious laughter drifted down the staircase. They were upstairs. His legs galloped up the stairs, taking them two and three at a time. Jealousy overwhelmed him. He burst into Echo's bedroom, flinging the door open with such force that the knob bounced off of the wainscoting sending the door rebounding back towards his face. He kicked it open again for good measure.

A startled Echo whirled around from her desk chair, her fingers curled over the computer's keyboard. The cable man stood behind her, leaning over with one hand on the mouse, his eyes wide and jaw open.

"Sorry to interrupt your bogey little tea party, but I think the lady has to be somewhere. Don't you Echo?" Flynn's words were coated with indignation.

"He…he," Echo stammered. "He was just showing me how to set up my email."

"Oh, he was, was he? *Was* is the bloody right word, and now he is done. Aren't you, you bowsie bugger?"

The cable man backed away and hurriedly began to gather his things. "Yeah, I…I think I'm finished here."

"You can bet your mutt's nuts you are!" Flynn concluded.

The cable man cautiously edged past Flynn, trying not to make eye or any other form of physical contact. His footsteps pounded on the stairs as he sprinted for the nearest exit.

"Flynn," Echo protested, "what is all of this about? I was just having my services hooked up."

"Oh, I see…your *services!* Since when does it take two bleepin' hours to have your *services* hooked up?"

"Well, I'll be damned, Flynn," Echo chuckled. "You're jealous."

Echo walked towards Flynn, slipping her arms around his waist.

"Awww, come on, don't be jealous. There's nothing to worry about here."

Jealousy…the word stabbed his gut with the sharpness of a double-edged dagger. He was discovering that it was one of his grievous faults, along with impetuosity and rashly jumping to conclusions. Faced with situations that were unfamiliar to him, he found that he couldn't always deal with them calmly. It was his nature to feel things more deeply than the mortals who surrounded him here. He wasn't used to reining in his emotions, especially these newly-discovered, love-induced negative ones.

He would look like a fool to her if he admitted that his hot head and wild imagination had brought him here. Not to mention, his outrageous jealousy could render him irrevocably unattractive to her. So, he reverted to what he knew she responded to—domination.

"Jealousy hasn't a bloody thing to do with it, Echo. What part of me being your Master don't you understand?"

Echo removed her arms from Flynn's waist, set her jaw and plopped down on the bed, her arms folded over her chest. "I didn't think having my cable installed had to be cleared with you!"

"*Everything* you do has to be cleared with me! That's the whole point of this arrangement. I thought you understood that. I tell you what to do, and when to do it. That's what you want, isn't it?" "Yes," Echo conceded with a sigh. "I just…I didn't think…" The corners of Echo's mouth turned down. Her chin quivered as she blinked back the tears welling from her eyes.

"Oh Sweet Jaysus, lass, don't start cryin' now."

He couldn't have screwed this up any more if he had tried. The hot brand of guilt burned in his chest. Castigating her didn't make him feel like a man, it made him feel like an ass. Barely one day into this arrangement, and he had fucked up royally. She should have kicked his sorry ass out of her house, but instead, she was looking to him for forgiveness.

He didn't dare look her in the eye. She didn't want some wimpy bowl of emotional jelly, she wanted a man who was strong and sure, and right now he felt anything but.

She was confused. Why wouldn't she be? He hadn't ever told her what he expected. Until now, he hadn't actually thought about it himself. Breathing deeply, he tried to dispel the nausea that was growing in his stomach.

He hoped there was still a chance to repair the damage. Tentatively, he moved near her, and, as he did, her emotions rushed into him and he felt her sorrow and confusion with such acuity that it pressed upon him like a leaden weight.

Wrapping her in his arms, he stroked her luxurious hair. She was a grown woman, but inside she was just a little girl who was scared, and falling in love for the first time. "There, there, lassie" he soothed. "I am so very sorry. I realize that you're still learning…and so am I."

"I'm sorry, too, Flynn." Echo choked. "It's all just happening so fast."

Seeing her beautiful face turn red and blotchy from the tears that he had caused tied Flynn's stomach into knots.

"We'll get it right. You'll see. All in good time," he cooed. "Now please, for the love of God, stop cryin'."

Flynn placed tiny butterfly kisses on her eyelids, tasting the salt that the tears had left behind. He kissed her forehead, her cheeks, the tip of her nose and then her mouth. A feeling more tender than he had ever known swelled in his breast, while a seed of doubt nagged at his soul. If he couldn't even handle a few tears, how was he ever going to fulfill his promise to her? What a delicate line they had chosen to walk. It was easy to provide the domination that she craved during sex; it came so naturally that he barely had to think about it. It was all the other times that had him completely confounded.

Assuming the Position

Echo awoke to the sound of a garbage truck clattering its way down the brick street. She stretched her arm behind her, drowsily feeling for Flynn, but the spot where he had lain was now empty. He had cradled her through the night; spooning against her while she slept. Several times she had felt the heat of his rigid cock pressing against her backside, but he had made no move towards using it on her. Not that she would have minded. Every minute that she was with him she was in such a heightened state of sexual arousal, fucking him was nearly all she could think about.

Working her hand inside of her panties, she reflected back on their encounter in the dressing room and rubbed her waking pussy.

As she stroked her dampening folds, she thought about how Flynn had burst into her room, breathless and with the veins nearly popping out of his neck. He had denied it, but he had been jealous alright. His jealousy actually turned her on. It was nice to have someone that cared about her enough to be jealous, even if it was a bit over the top.

She could almost come right now just thinking about him. If he had that much passion inside of him, just imagine what he'd be like making love! The thought stilled her hand. If they were going to have sex later, she didn't want to dull her passion. She wanted her body to be on fire for him. Echo rolled out of bed, blinking the lethargy from her eyes. A note, suspended from a piece of tape, fluttered on her computer screen. Echo crossed the room and sat down to read.

"Good morning, sexy. I hope you slept well because you're going to need to be well rested. I want to tell you that I assume the responsibility for our misunderstanding yesterday. I should have set my expectations for you from the start.

Although I require your complete and total submission, I have no interest in running all the aspects of your daily life, unless you tell me that is what you want. However, if I tell you to dress a certain way, or wear a certain shade of lipstick, that is my prerogative and you will comply.

I require your utter truthfulness and honesty. There will be no withholding of any *requested* information, period. That includes information about personal relationships between you and other people.

Be advised, as your Master, I not only own you, but I own your relationships with others as well. I will not interfere in those relationships as long as they do not interfere with ours, and I request, that for the time being, we keep our relationship private.

We are going to be taking things up a notch, and I promise to keep you safe, no matter how deeply you may get lost in your submission.

You are my friend, my lover and my most sacred possession.

That being said, here are your instructions for the day: You may go about your normal business. I want you to eat a substantial breakfast because I fear that you do not always remember to eat, and I do not want you to lose that round, luscious ass of yours.

I want you to keep your contact with the outside world to a minimum.

Instead, reflect on what you have learned in order to prepare yourself for what's to come.

At precisely six o'clock, you are to stop whatever you are doing, shower once again; paying special attention to assure that the whole of your body smells sweet. Apply makeup and the perfume of your choice. Wear your hair in a free-flowing fashion; do not tie it up or pile it on top of your head. Dress yourself. I have already selected what you will be wearing. You will find it hanging on the door of your closet. At seven-thirty, go to Barney Dillon's Pub. There has been a table reserved in your name. Order two pints. Ever, Flynn"

So there it was, all set in black and white, the parameters of his expectations made clear. Stretching across the bed, she read the note once more. It was exactly what she needed. No more guessing, and hopefully no more surprise enraged visits from Flynn.

Now that she knew the good from the bad, Echo felt more confident that she wouldn't make the same error she had yesterday. She did not want to disappoint him ever again.

She liked that she didn't have to make any decisions; he would make them all for her. It was almost like being a child again, where mommy and daddy took care of the big, bad world, and all she had to do was try her best to be a good... well, and bad... girl.

* * *

Echo passed the day as Flynn had instructed. Several times when the house seemed especially quiet, voices had filtered in and out of her consciousness, but they were faint and garbled. She debated when it might be a good time to tell Flynn about her "gift". For the time being, she didn't think it necessary to reveal her secret to him. The letter had said there would be no withholding of requested information. He didn't say anything about embarrassing, dark secrets that he knew nothing of. Plus, she didn't want to spoil the fun that they were having.

The clock crawled through the hours. As she went about her business, Echo imagined what Flynn might have in store for her. He said they were going to take it up a notch. Would tonight be the night he made love to her? He had kept her in a state of constant craving. She was fierce with curiosity regarding his lovemaking. Plus, his sizeable cock held the promise of a fuck that she would not soon forget. When he finally shared her bed, would she be able to hold back the feelings she had for him or would they come rushing out in the heat of passion?

The nearer to six o'clock the hands crept, the more Echo's anticipation grew. By the instant the chimes rang six times, Echo was sliding off the edge of her seat and so sexually stirred up that she thought she might not last the next hour without "taking care of business." But she didn't. She wanted to save every last drop of herself for Flynn.

Echo applied her makeup. She wasn't one to wear layers of cosmetics. Her ivory skin was freckled, but clear and smooth. She lined her large green eyes with amethyst, which showcased them to perfection. Echo chose a neutral gloss for her lips, dabbing a touch of highlighter on the center of her bottom lip. It picked up the light, imparting a sexy pout to her mouth. *Let's see if he can resist these gorgeous lips.*

From her arsenal of perfumes, she selected the sultriest scent, choosing to dab a bit between her legs as well as her neck and cleavage.

Echo had made a point not to look into the closet until she was ready to dress. Now checking, she found that Flynn had decided on her aqua blue halter dress with the empire waist and flirty skirt that shimmied around her hips when she walked. Her slinky silver peep-toe pumps had been pulled from their box and now sat on the floor of the closet. There were no undergarments. Was she to assume that was how he wanted it? Erring on the side of caution she decided to put on only what he had laid out.

Time was running short. Echo stepped into the dress, tied the halter around her neck and slipped her feet into the pumps. Standing before the mirror, she checked herself from different angles. She knew that she turned heads. With her long legs, curvy form and thick curls, she had always attracted attention. She wasn't concerned what anyone else thought of her; tonight she only cared that Flynn found her irresistible.

* * *

Echo strolled into the pub, an inviting spot with old wood, worn brass and antique wavy glass in the windows.

The atmosphere was comfortably lively. It was still early as far as nightlife was concerned, and the pub had not yet gone into full swing. The bar was more than half full. A few diners were scattered about at tables and booths.

As the waiter showed her to a corner booth, Echo attracted attention. Men and women alike stopped what they were doing to admire the stunning redhead.

Echo ordered two pints of Guinness and waited. She hadn't eaten since breakfast and the aroma from the kitchen caused her stomach to growl in protest.

The waiter set the pints on the table, asking if she wanted to order. Echo declined, explaining that she was waiting for someone. Truthfully, she *guessed* that she was waiting for Flynn. She really didn't know what to expect.

At precisely seven forty-five Flynn burst into the room. Shouts of hello rang out through the pub. Flynn waved and called greetings to some of the patrons while making his way to the table. He was about as handsome as Echo could stand. A tailored white, button down shirt fit him like a second skin. Black, flat front trousers, with creases so sharp they looked like they might do damage if he crossed his legs, ended with a perfect break over his leather loafers. A hint of a five o'clock shadow whiskered his face, imparting him with a roguish charm. Echo was envious. He was more beautiful than she.

He slid into the booth and sidled up to Echo. He was in a jovial mood and smiling broadly.

"Mmmm," he hummed, kissing Echo on the neck. "You look banging hot."

"So do you." Echo put her hand on his muscled thigh. She couldn't keep her paws off of him when he was this close to her.

Flynn picked up his pint and drained it in one draught, thumping the empty glass on the table. A bit of foam remained on his upper lip. Echo pointed at it.

"You have some foam…"

"Why don't you lick it off of me," he suggested shrugging his eyebrows.

Echo licked the pungent brew from his mouth with the tip of her tongue. From the corner of her eye she saw several people watching her. She decided to give them their money's worth, and brazenly sucked his upper lip into her mouth, licking the last traces of the Guinness from his skin. Embarrassed, the onlookers averted their gaze.

The waiter stood by the table clearing his throat. "Are you ready to order?"

Flynn pulled away from Echo's seductive mouth. "Lord, yes we are. I'm so hungry I could eat a baby's arse through the bars of a cot. Bring me another pint, better make that two pints… and the lady will have the shepherd's pie and I would like the whiskey baked ham."

"It'll be up in a few," advised the server.

Flynn turned his attention to Echo. "So, how was your day? Did you do everything you should've and nothing that you shouldn't?"

"I did my best."

"That's a good girl." Flynn's fingers walked up Echo's thigh and under her dress. "So far, so good." she replied coyly.

His fingers inched further, grazing the soft strip of hair hidden beneath the folds of her dress. Echo uncrossed her legs, careful to not draw attention to their public display of affection.

Two more pints appeared on the table. The waiter was giving Flynn a wide berth. He was trying to do his job and be as invisible as possible so as not to intrude on the lovers.

Flynn's finger located her clit and was now teasing her to distraction.

"Miss me?" Echo tried to keep her eyes from rolling back into her head. Damn, she felt like straddling him and riding his cock right there in the booth. She battled between maintaining her composure and surrendering to Flynn's seduction. She took a long pull on the tall glass, attempting to act nonchalant. "Mmmhmm," was all she could manage to reply.

Flynn nuzzled her face and pressed his mouth against her ear. "Hungry?"

The tickle of his mouth on her ear shivered down her spine. "Ravenous," she replied, clutching the spongy firmness of his testicles. The kitchen door swung open and the server headed their way with the steaming entrees. Flynn removed his hand from under Echo's dress.

The waiter set the plates on the table. Flynn put his fingers near his nose and sniffed. "Smells delicious, I can't wait to dig in."

The food smelled scrumptious and she was starving, but Echo couldn't help but resent the poor timing of it. She wanted to hurry through the meal so they could get back to more under-the-table play. She was practically crawling out of her skin with sexual arousal. Despite her hunger, if she had the choice of filling her mouth with shepherd's pie or Flynn's tongue, his tongue was the hands down winner. "Bad boy" Flynn was most appealing. Echo loved how he thumbed his nose in the face of acceptable behavior. There was an element of danger beneath Flynn's surface; Echo had learned firsthand that danger was a powerful aphrodisiac. Dinner was delightful. When Flynn said to eat, Echo ate, grateful to be filling the vacancy in her stomach. She spoke when she was spoken to, and she found it to be a welcome relief. It was a pleasant change to be entertained and not be the one who kept the conversation flowing.

Flynn did most of the talking. He prattled on about a room in his house he had been doing some remodeling on. He talked about how crisp the weather had been that day. He told her that he had been missing her every minute, and how it helped him to know exactly what she was doing when he wasn't with her.

The pub grew more raucous as the dinner crowd departed and the space filled with thirsty patrons. An Irish folk band took the stage with a rousing rendition of *Bog Down in the Valley*. Echo and Flynn sang along with the others, swaying their pints in time to the music.

"O-ro the rattlin' bog, the bog down in the valley-o O-ro the rattlin' bog, the bog down in the valley-o"

Several songs into the band's set, a chair was sent flying from somewhere in the far corner of the bar and a scuffle ensued. Trying to make his voice heard over the commotion, Flynn bellowed,

"We best be on our way, looks as if there's about to be a Millie up." "A Millie what?" Echo shouted back.

"A fight, a fight…fisticuffs!" he replied over the din.

Flynn paid the tab, leaving a more than generous tip.

"Come on," he urged, ushering Echo towards the exit. "Let's move along."

Echo searched her purse for the keys to her Mini Cooper.

"Those won't be necessary. We're staying in town tonight. We can walk." Flynn held the pub door open, beckoning Echo into the crisp night air. The moon was waning and only a sliver remained suspended in the starry sky. Echo shivered, rubbing the goose bumps on her arms.

"Sorry," he said, shielding her from the cold with his arm. "I made a balls of your clothing and neglected to give you a coat. Oh, well, we'll be there soon enough and warming our tits and toes by the fire."

Echo didn't know where they were headed, and had decided not to care. For now it was enough to know that he had a plan and it included her. She was along for the ride, wherever it might lead. Instead of questioning and fretting, she could relax totally in the moment and just enjoy the lively sounds of the street, the glittering lights in the sky, and the feel of their bodies moving in unison along the pavement. For the first time in a long time, she felt truly alive.

True to his word, they only strolled a city block before Flynn guided her into the gleaming brass-trimmed doors of the historic Park Hotel. Echo loved fancy hotels: the imported linens, room service brought on silver-domed trays, and the plush complimentary terry robes that made her feel pampered and special.

"Oh, this place is so extravagant!" She exclaimed bouncing up and down on her heels as Flynn led her toward the elevator.

"Life is short, kiddo, pay an extra dime and go first class is what I always say. I wasn't sure if you would like this or if you were more the B&B type. I hope I made the right choice."

Like it? She loved it! It was fantastic. Echo rose on her tiptoes, placing a kiss on his cheek. "You definitely made the right choice."

The elevator doors opened, and they stepped into the mirrored interior. Flynn pressed the number fifteen button, the doors closed, cocooning them into the small space, and the elevator whirred towards its destination.

Echo's curiosity was peeked. "What's all this about?" She probed.

"You have been a very good girl today and you deserve something special." Flynn promised. "Remember, good girls are rewarded and bad girls are punished."

A reward? Echo was already as giddy as if she had won the lottery.

She was having so much fun that she felt up to anything that he might have in store for her…especially if included hot sex in a luxury hotel. She was hoping to be a good girl in a very bad way.

Flynn positioned himself behind Echo, turning her to face the mirror.

Her chilly nipples poked through the silk dress like two prize pearls. The elevator hummed towards its destination, vibrating beneath her feet.

Flynn glided his hands along her waist and over her hips. The muscles of her abdomen tightened and jumped at his touch. She gazed into his eyes reflected in the mirror image as he walked his fingers down her thighs until he reached the hem of her dress. Curling his fingers over the fabric he gathered it inch by inch in his hands, raising it ever higher.

Echo's eyes darted briefly to the long panel of elevator buttons. The number fifteen remained the single lit button. She prayed no one would call the elevator and interrupt their naughty party.

As the elevator ascended, musak filtered through a speaker and Flynn hummed along, his mouth so near to Echo's ear that the vibration of his humming rippled on her skin.

"Fly me to the moon and let me play among the stars."

Echo observed in the mirror while Flynn kissed her neck and petted the downy strip between her legs. She was torn between wanting the elevator ride to go on forever and yearning for it to stop so she could race to their room, rip off her clothes and fuck him senseless.

His fingers didn't probe. He merely stroked and pressed the wet triangle between her legs, skimming his fingertips through the curly golden red hairs, an occasional finger lightly grazing her swelling clit. The slow, measured movements were maddeningly arousing. Her knees were weakening and she felt like sinking to the floor. She reached her arms backward, grasping Flynn's firm ass, pressing him closely to her. As she steadied her body against him, the rigid line of his cock nudged against the small of her back. Echo hoped it was a signal that tonight was the night that he would share his elusive manhood with her.

The elevator jerked to a sudden stop. Flynn quickly smoothed her dress back into place. She was still holding him tightly against her as the doors parted. Flynn's reflection grinned at her as he shrugged his eyebrows suggestively.

"This is our floor," he announced, extricating himself from her hungry grasp. Leading her by the hand, they padded noiselessly down the carpeted hallway. Echo's heart fluttered more rapidly with each step as they approached room fifteen-o-four.

The suite was lovely and well-appointed in Beaux Arts fashion. Echo couldn't resist eyeing the large, comfortable bed. She had to admit, the man had class.

"Do you have to go to the bathroom?" Flynn asked.

"Oh, I thought you would never ask. Yes, I do."

"Go on then. Take off your clothes while you're at it."

Echo excused herself and stripped down in the bathroom, folding her dress neatly on the vanity stool and leaving her shoes in the corner. What did Flynn have planned for her tonight? Her hands were trembling slightly. She balled them up into tight fists, opening and closing them, trying to shake loose the tension.

She dampened a washcloth, dabbing it along her neck.

Control yourself. Let him do his thing, she reminded. *Don't be so anxious to jump to the finish line...just calm down and remember to do what you're told. He promised to take you places that you never imagined...so just let him.*

Echo smoothed her hair and rinsed out her mouth. After eliminating several pints of ale, she wetted a washcloth and scrupulously cleaned her nether regions which were already juicy with anticipation. A fresh coat of lip gloss, a spritz of perfume, and Echo squared her shoulders, ready for the unknown.

Flynn was standing in the same spot as when she had left—his arms folded across his chest. The blue of his eyes darkened slightly and his pupils widened with a hungry intensity.

"Come closer." He pointed at a spot on the floor a few feet in front of him.

Echo approached, stopping at the indicated location.

"I am going to teach you the correct way to present yourself to me. I want you to move from one position to the next with fluidity. Your postures should be graceful." *Postures? Just like Yoga.* Echo thought. *I can do this.*

Flynn's talk of postures and presenting herself to him reminded her that this was the real deal...hard core dom/sub stuff. She needed to do this right, prove to him that she was capable of following his lead. If he wanted her on her knees, she would drop so fast it would amaze him. If he wanted her on her back, she would lie at his feet, looking up at his cock and savor every minute of it.

"Turn around, face away from me. Drop to your hands and knees, with your knees shoulder width apart."

Echo knew this position. It was the same as Yoga's dog-tilt pose. She also knew how to appear stunningly sexy in this pose which was an exhibitionists dream come true. It was difficult to believe that she was actually doing this! But here she was, in this gorgeous hotel suite, living out her fantasy…and she wanted to make everything go just right.

Slowly, she glided the toes of her right foot backward along the carpet until her knee found the floor. She straightened her foot until the top of it rested on the smooth fibers of the carpet. She repeated the movements with her left leg, positioning her knees so that they were just below her hips. Coming into the pose, a strange sense of reverence descended on her. Until now she hadn't realized that being a submissive wasn't merely a role to take on and off; it was more a feeling, a state of being. And despite the outward appearance, it was a place of power. Although she couldn't see them, she had the distinct feeling that Flynn's eyes were boring into her, his arousal blossoming as she performed the ritual. This was a new kind of foreplay, both mental and physical, and more deeply intimate than groping hands and hungry mouths.

One at a time, Echo lowered her hands lightly to the floor, her fingers spread. She made certain that her shoulders didn't sag into the position, but instead were held strongly open, supported by the sinewy muscles of her arms. Deeply dipping her spine, she tilted her pelvis towards the ceiling, providing Flynn a stunning view of her pouting pussy. Echo looked over her shoulder at Flynn for approval, certain that he would be salivating at the sight of her upturned ass.

"Don't look at me," he admonished. "Keep your head down. Look only at my shoes."

Echo cringed at his reprimand and lowered her gaze to the floor. It was her first mistake and it stung. Just when she had been feeling puffed up with pride, certain he was standing with his tongue lolling out of his mouth, he had reminded her that he could and would resist her if he chose to. She would have to work a little harder, try not to do anything to offend, and allow his arousal to build as his dominance over her increased.

Flynn circled her body, dragging his hand lightly along the curve of her buttocks and back, inspecting her like a prize piece of horse-flesh. Echo's confidence waned. She became nervous about her flaws, the small scar on her thigh, the extra bit of weight on her hips, she wondered if the bottoms of her feet were dirty.

Standing in front of her, he placed his palm on her head, as if in blessing. "You please me very much."

Echo exhaled a sigh of relief.

She followed his feet with her eyes as he walked menacingly once more around her kneeling form. His pacing focused her senses. Her ears tuned acutely to the measured beat of his footsteps.

Echo's arms began to burn. How long was he going to keep her in this pose?

Flynn came to rest behind her, stepping between her legs and leaning his knees against her buttocks. "Who is your Master?" he asked in a sotto, measured tone.

The question took Echo by surprise. He was testing her, seeing if she knew the correct answer. She wasn't certain how she was supposed to answer, but she took a stab at it.

"You are."

Flynn rapidly fired another query. "To whom do you belong?"

Oh good, she must have gotten it right.

"To you, I belong to you."

"Very good, you are doing very well." His voice was little more than a whisper now. Echo had to tune her ears keenly to hear his words. Flynn's hand passed so lightly over her buttocks that is caused the hairs on the back of her neck to stand on end. An odd mixture of nervous agitation and forbidden pleasure put her body on a state of alert. The slightest touch was multiplied, every sensation heightened.

The nervousness had melted away. The pacing, his emotionless, methodical manner of speaking, the carefully orchestrated tactile sensations; all served to still her mind and focus her attention. She sensed, no, she could actually *feel*, Flynn's energy emanating through his clothing and melding with hers.

"To whom do you give your power?"

"I give my power to you," Echo whispered automatically.

"Louder. I can't hear you…don't mumble. If you give your power to me, then declare it." Flynn pinched her upturned ass.

Echo clenched her muscles against the sharp pain. A quickening stirred inside of her. She became acutely aware of gravity tugging at her breasts as they swayed below her. Flynn's knees pressed into her ass, forcing her juices to ooze from her nether lips. She burned for him to own her, to possess her, to release her from this wicked torment.

"I give my power to you," she panted.

"Well done. You may release the pose and kneel in an upright position. Do not sit back on your heels."

Echo raised her body, but not her eyes, which she mindfully maintained in a downcast position. She wanted to rub the burn from her arm muscles, but instead clasped her hands dutifully behind her back. When her knees came together, creamy nectar dampened her thighs.

Flynn stood in front of her. Although Echo's eyes were focused downward, her peripheral vision saw his engorged prick, bulging beneath the fabric of his pants. She unconsciously licked her lips.

Flynn pressed his hand to the back of her head and urged her face into his crotch. His erection pulsed against her flushed cheek. She longed to free his cock and know the taste of him. She clasped her hands more tightly behind her back, digging her nails into her flesh to control them. She buried her nose in Flynn's crotch, inhaling the sharp scent of his testicles. The aroma triggered her lust and, like Pavlov's dog, her pussy salivated at the smell.

After a moment, Flynn released her head. Cupping her chin in his hand, he lifted her face to look at him.

"Exceptional," he praised. "You've earned a small reward."

Flynn had worked her into a state of near delirium. Echo was barely cognizant of her surroundings. The only sound she was attuned to was the sound of his voice.

Pointing to a chair he commanded, "Crawl to that chair, sit in it and present your wet pussy to me.

Echo crawled across the floor like a cat, her hips swaying sensually with each stretching movement. The carpet stung her knees as she dragged towards the chair.

Obediently, she stood erect, and positioned herself upon the ivory upholstered chair, languorously draping her legs over the gilded arms. She had never displayed herself so unashamedly to anyone but her gynecologist. She had never considered her twat as her most attractive asset. Viewings this intimate usually involved very low lighting, but the way Flynn looked at her, as if it was the most sublime vision he had ever seen, emboldened her. She wanted him to see the results of his efforts. How his words and touch had drenched her with arousal. She wanted him to see her swollen labia pleading for his caress. She wanted to tease him with the promise of her warm, tight pussy beckoning to be invaded by his cock. So brazenly, she exhibited her most private parts, daring him to resist.

Flynn unfastened his cufflinks. They made a tinkling sound as he dropped them into a small porcelain dish. He pulled his shirttails from his pants, casually unbuttoned his shirt and removed it. His chest glistened with perspiration. Echo was impressed with the control he exerted. She was practically crawling out of her skin and she marveled that he could appear so relaxed.

Echo's gaze drifted toward his magnificent member straining at his zipper. Flynn unbuckled his belt and removed it from the loops in a single swift motion. His growing erection must have caused some discomfort because he also released the top button of his trousers. The bulbous head of his straining cock protruded from his waistband. A single drop of pre-ejaculate shimmered like mercury on its tip.

Flynn walked round the rear of the chair, snapping his belt so it made a cracking sound. Echo twitched with each ear-splitting clap of the leather. He lifted her arms, stretching them behind the chair. A strap tightened around her left wrist, another around her right. Her palms met in a single sharp movement, stretching her breastbone. The belt buckle jangled as Flynn cinched the restraint. His finger slipped between her skin and the leather that bound her, checking that it wasn't too tight.

She was vulnerable, helpless, and approaching a fever-pitch of desire. She did her best to maintain a cool exterior as she focused on her breasts, watching them rise and fall with her breathing. Her nipples puckered in the cool air.

The heated skin of Flynn's palms crawled down her neck, and over her shoulders. Her eyes followed his finely sculpted hands as he trailed them over her chest, and cupped her breasts. At his longed-for touch, she arched her back, pressing her heavy tits into his hands. She studied his hands as they kneaded her breasts. They were beautiful; long, sculpted fingers, finely boned, blue veins prominent beneath his tawny skin.

His thumbs stroked her tingling nipples and they sprouted into full erection. She writhed beneath his touch, savoring his skin against her flesh.

"Mmmm…your Master loves your big, round tits. Perhaps one day I'll fuck them. Would you like that?"

Hell, yes she would like that. Echo imagined slurping the head of his cock in and out of her mouth while he fucked her tits.

"Yes," she moaned, "I'd like that very much."

"Someday, but not tonight—tonight is for you."

Flynn's right hand crawled teasingly down her abdomen towards her pussy. Echo's stomach quivered and jumped as his hand passed.

Flynn's breath was in her ear. His whiskers stabbed at the tender skin on her cheek. Warm lips on her neck, kisses soft as eiderdown raining onto her flesh like rose-petals, she felt all of these things.

"Would you like to know what your reward is?" he whispered.

Echo watched his index finger circling her clitoris. It didn't matter what her reward was as long as he kept touching her.

"Oh, yes, please," she pleaded.

"Your reward is an Aussie Kiss."

It was a new term for Echo. "What's an Aussie Kiss, Master?"

"It's like a French Kiss," Flynn penetrated her pussy with his finger, "but down under!" Echo's head swooned to the back of the chair. With all of her might, she gripped his probing finger with her muscles, squeezing it inside of her and raising her hips from the chair.

"Thank you, Master," she exclaimed.

"You may make as much noise as you wish; in fact, I insist that you tell me how much you like it when I eat your horny little honeypot."

Flynn came to the front of the chair and positioned himself on his knees between Echo's outstretched legs. He shrugged his eyebrows suggestively, displaying a cock-eyed grin. He greedily licked his lips.

Echo closed her eyes in ecstatic anticipation. She knew that she wouldn't last long. The moment that she felt the warm wetness of Flynn's tongue against her clit, her abdomen tensed, her legs involuntarily twitched and her climax burst forth, nearly tipping the chair onto its back legs. Even while in the throes of orgasm, she heard her voice begging for more.

"Don't stop, please, don't stop," she pleaded.

"Do you like it when I lick your cunt?" Flynn teased.

"I love it when you lick my cunt. Please do it again." Echo moved her legs to wrap them around Flynn's neck and push his face into her dripping bush, but Flynn forced them back on top of the chair arms.

"Keep your legs in place. I enjoy looking at your slippery snatch."

Flynn's fingers traced the pink folds. "So luscious, so tempting, so ripe." Flynn flattened his tongue and lapped her from back to front.

Echo recoiled slightly when his tongue reached her still throbbing clit.

She hadn't imagined it could be this good. At first she thought that having her hands restrained would just be a fun game, but now she realized that not being able to move her body allowed her to focus more intently on Flynn's touch.

When he sucked her clit into his mouth, she cried out in ecstasy. "Oh, God, that's it. Tell me I'm a good girl, Master...say it, please." "You're a good girl," Flynn answered. He pushed two fingers inside of her, stroking her G-spot. "with a bad, hungry little pussycat."

Echo's head thrashed to and fro. The pressure Flynn applied to her G-spot caused her to bear down on his fingers, crushing and entrapping them inside of her.

Flynn's tongue flicked over her protruding jewel, his fingers strumming the spot just behind her pubic bone. Echo became dizzy. She felt an unusual sensation, almost as if she was going to urinate, and then it came—an incredible feeling of release roaring from her loins, followed by an ejaculation of juices erupting from deep within her that overwhelmed the whole of her being. Echo heard someone wailing in the distance, a tortured cry of unintelligible sounds. Then she realized the sound was coming from her own throat. She slumped into the cushions, euphoric and spent. The words rushed out from her lips, as unstoppable and unbridled as her climax. "I love you, Flynn" she panted. "I love you. God help me, I do."

Echo's Indiscretion

"Wakey, Wakey, eggs and bakey!" Flynn clapped his hands together loudly.

Echo stirred beneath the down coverlet, sinking her head more deeply into the pillow.

"No," she mumbled, "…too early."

Damn, this woman is exasperating! Flynn got down on one knee and whispered into her ear. "If you don't get up this very instant, I am going to pick you up by your short hairs and make you sit in the corner while I eat breakfast."

Flynn pulled the covers from her body. Echo rolled onto her back, blinking at him. The sight of her buxom figure and tousled rusty hair caused his prick to twitch. He was about as pent up with sexual frustration as any man could be. He wanted to pounce on top her, force his way between her legs, bury his cock to the hilt inside of her eager pussy and fuck her until she begged him to stop. Unfortunately he had stupidly forgotten to pack…what were those torturous things…oh, yes, condoms.

They were a definite drawback of the mortal realm. Not that he had to worry about any of the dreadful diseases that plagued mankind, but one taste, one drop of his semen in her body would cause a reaction that would raise questions he wasn't prepared to answer just yet.

He turned from her to regain his composure. He wasn't going to be able to hold out for much longer. He was going to have to find a way to tell her about himself, and soon. He couldn't think straight when she was around. She was too great a distraction. He needed to get her safely back home and then he could contemplate his next move. He was in a race against time and he had to stay one step ahead of the ticking clock, and one step ahead of her. If he could keep her on the defensive, keep her guessing, he might be able to hold her questions at bay until he figured out where to go from here.

"Just stop being difficult and get out of bed. Room service has brought us a delicious breakfast and I want you to sit down and enjoy it with me. I don't think that is too much to ask."

Echo rolled her eyes, slid out of bed, shuffled her naked body over to the table and seated herself with a plop.

Flynn dropped his head, trying not to show his irritation. What else could he do? She awakened in this spectacular room, to a perfectly lovely breakfast and she obviously felt as if it were some terrible torture he was subjecting her to. He wondered if she was always this grumpy when she woke up.

"You are obviously *not* a morning person," Flynn observed. He sat opposite her, placing his napkin tidily in his lap. Echo only pursed her lips in response and stared dully at her place setting.

Maybe she didn't feel well. "Have a headache?" he probed.

Echo pressed a finger to her eyebrow and curtly replied, "No."

"Well, I can't read your mind, darlin'. How about some coffee…a little caffeine kick to get the blood pumping." Flynn lifted the silver pot and poured the steaming coffee into her cup, praying that a few sips would change her mood.

With the tip of her finger, Echo pushed the cup and saucer to the middle of the table, plopped her chin into the palm of hand and stared off into space.

A stinging dart of pain began to nag at Flynn's temple. He ran over the details of everything that had happened the night before and for the life of him, he couldn't figure out what was bothering her. Her brows were knitted and the corners of her mouth turned down. She looked like a teenager who had just been told they couldn't borrow the car.

"Stop pouting. I mean it, Echo. Get that pout off of your face. It's very unpleasant."

Echo mocked him, shooting a simpering smile in his direction.

He was out of guesses and out of patience.

"Alright," he said, slamming his fork on the table, the dishes rattling in the wake. "What beetle is crawling around *your* tall grass today? What could have possibly happened between last night and this morning that has put you in such a foul mood? Come on, out with it."

"Nothing," she deferred.

Nothing, my ass. What a load of blarney. Her face was sullen, she refused to eat or drink. He had hoped to be greeted with a big kiss and the same gush of girlish excitement he had seen in her last night when he'd brought her to this place. Instead, she sat across from him with her lips pressed so tightly together that the blood had drained from them.

"Look, Echo, I am not playing that buggery game, so don't even try. What is going on with you this morning?"

Echo sighed and played with her food, pushing it around her plate, making annoying scraping noises with her fork. Several times she looked up at him and opened her mouth as if she were going to speak, but then would drop her head again. Now, turning a sugar packet over and over in her hand, she stammered.

"It's just...I thought...I thought that last night you were going to... oh, never mind. Forget about it."

"Forget about it?" Flynn was at his wit's end. "I don't even bloody know what it is I am supposed to forget *about!* Spit it out, Echo. Last night I was going to...what?"

Echo flicked the sugar packet with her finger, punting it across the room. "Okay! Last night I thought you were finally going to make love to me."

The spark had returned to her eyes and they now flared with indignant intensity. She crossed her arms over her chest, settling against the back of the chair with finality. "There I said it. But you didn't, and I don't know why."

Flynn inwardly cringed. So, that was it. He was afraid this would come up sooner or later. Of course she wanted him to make love to her, it only made sense. Hadn't he set the expectation for it to happen last night...the dinner, the room?

"I am beginning to think that you don't desire me. Don't you want me like I want you?" Her voice had taken on a childlike whine. Her eyes implored for an answer.

"My God, of course I do." Flynn reached across the table, reaching for her hand. She kept her arms folded resolutely over her chest and stared down at the eggs that were growing cold on her plate.

She must think I am some sort of a freak or something, or worse—that I can't perform.

Flynn lowered his voice to a soothing tone, "I have my reasons. It has nothing to do with how beautiful you are, or my desire for you. You have no idea how bloody hard it has been for me to hold back. My balls are turning blue. Last night, when you climaxed, I shot my wad all over my knickers."

Echo chewed on her lower lip. "You did?"

"Yes, and thank God that I did, otherwise my nuts would be swollen to the size of soccer balls."

Echo turned her face to the side, her eyes narrowing in suspicion. "So exactly why didn't you make love to me?"

How was he going to gracefully extricate himself from this interrogation? He could confess the whole truth, but she was already beside herself. He had made so many blunders since the start of this he couldn't risk blurting, "Oh, hey, by the way, I'm not like you. In fact, I'm nearly another species entirely, and I have this big dark secret that I've hidden from you, but go ahead now and enjoy your breakfast!" In the emotional state they were both in, it could easily escalate into a very ugly scene.

Flynn pushed his chair out and patted his knee. "Come here. Sit."

Reluctantly, she scooted her chair away from the table. Her face softened ever so slightly as she approached. Flynn stretched his arms out in invitation. Finally, she acquiesced, curling into his lap, her arms encircling his shoulders. He kissed her neck, and ran his hand over the silky skin of her breast. His cock tingled and grew turgid. Flynn placed Echo's hand over his burgeoning bulge. "See how much I want you?"

Echo's hand gripped his penis through his clothing, stroking its length. "As much as I want you?" she murmured.

"More." He taunted. *This woman is a handful. She has the sexual appetite of a mink. No matter what I give her, it isn't enough.*

"Please, Master," she coaxed. "May I please suck your big, thick cock? Just one taste and I promise I will stop—if you want me to."

Flynn considered the possibility. He considered pushing his prick between her moist, plump lips. He imagined her teasing tongue lapping at his swollen, aching head. He envisioned bending her over the large, springy bed and pounding his battering ram into her wet, willing pussy.

Flynn entrapped Echo's hand, removing it from his crotch, and raised it to his lips. Kissing the back of her hand, he declined. "Not this time, lass. The thing is…I'm a bit embarrassed to admit…I thought I had everything planned out so well, but in my haste, I forgot to bring condoms." At least that was partially true. "I tried to do the best with the equipment I had at my disposal."

Finally, her face brightened and she beamed a smile in his direction.

The tension drained from her shoulders and she hugged her arms tightly around him. "I thought we covered that way back on the night we discussed jumping into this. Remember, after dinner I told you that I was on birth control and we both attested to having clean bills of health?"

Damnation, she had a good memory. "I must have forgotten...force of habit, I suppose." In truth, he wasn't in the habit of using a condom at all. How fortunate his world was sterile, where mating occurred without the threat of disease and death.

Echo was smiling again and all was right with the world...almost.

Flynn's stomach balled into a tight fist when he thought about his necessary deception. She deserved to know the whole truth, and Flynn resolved to tell her at the next opportunity.

A germ of a plan began to take root in his mind. What if the next time they were together, he provided her with an inkling of things to come? A drop or two on her tongue and certainly she would become aware that something was decidedly different about him. Not enough to effect any permanent changes in her physiology, but enough for her to begin to question him. With that small bit of proof, he might be able to convince her that he truly was what he said he was.

"Flynn, are you still with me?" Echo's fingers were snapping in front of his nose, rousing him from his rumination.

"I'm with you, baby...always." Flynn patted her bottom. "Now finish your breakfast like a good girl. Get washed and dressed and then I am taking you home."

* * *

Flynn saw Echo safely into the house. The boxes they had abandoned days before still sat in the foyer.

"May I check my phone messages?" Echo petitioned.

"Of course," Flynn replied offhandedly. "I'm going to take a few of these boxes upstairs for you. I feel like a right git leaving them for you to lift."

Echo excused herself and walked towards the kitchen. Flynn hoisted the box marked "Bedroom" onto his shoulder and trudged up the stairs to Echo's room. When he dropped the box to the floor, his leg bumped the computer desk. The screensaver dissolved and an Instant Message conversation, left over from the day before, appeared.

Flynn spied his name repeated in the lines of the message. She had been talking about him to someone!

Flynn quickly scanned the conversation: Blah, blah, blah, Flynn… blah, blah, blah, Master…blah, blah, blah…

He'd seen enough to know that he had to know more. Quickly hitting the print button, he peeled off the pages as they came from the printer one by one and stuffed them into his pants.

"Echo," he called dashing down the stairs, "I have something I just remembered that I have to do. I'll call you."

From the kitchen he heard her sing out a cheery, "Okay, see you later."

The door rattled behind him as he left.

* * *

Ensconced in the turret room, Flynn pulled the crumpled pages from his pants and sat down to examine them, his hands shaking as he read.

Chi-town Cutie: Hey, you're back on-line! How'ya doing, girlfriend?

Bravo Echo Tango: Couldn't be better. How's my best girl?

Chi-town Cutie: Missing you and our ladies night out. How's the new town? Meet anyone interesting?

Bravo Echo Tango: As a matter of fact, I have…a scrumptious neighbor named Flynn.

Chi-town Cutie: Details! Details!

Bravo Echo Tango: Number one, he's single, Number two, he's a gorgeous hunk of Irish masculinity. Number three, he's interested in me and I am interested in him in a big way.

Chi-town Cutie: Well that was super-fast! So have you….?

Bravo Echo Tango: Sort of. It's very, very scandalously sexual between us…but no actual "doing it" yet. It's a "different" sort of relationship.

Chi-town Cutie: Different? How different?

Bravo Echo Tango: Don't freak out when I tell you this, but Flynn and I are in what is called a Dominant/Submissive relationship.

Chi-town Cutie: He wants you to dominate him?

Bravo Echo Tango: The other way around. He dominates me…he's my master, and I love it.

Chi-Town Cutie: You're kidding me, right? You let this guy boss you around and tell you what to do? I can hardly believe that, Echo. How can you stand for it?

Bravo Echo Tango: It's not like that. Yeah, he tells me what to do;

as a matter of fact, I am not entirely sure I am supposed to be talking to you right now, but he does it because he knows it turns me on.

Flynn looked up from the pages, narrowing his eyes. His hand absentmindedly rubbed the hint of whiskers on his chin. Not entirely sure? Hadn't he made it clear in his instructions that she wasn't to talk to anyone about their relationship? He was certain he had mentioned that. So, was she picking and choosing what instructions she would follow?

The last thing he needed right now was one of her girlfriends snooping into his life, asking Echo questions about him that she hadn't yet thought of herself. What's his background...what's his family like... all the little details he'd been able to steer clear of so far.

Flynn paced tight, worried circles as he read.

Chi-town Cutie: So you get off on it?

Bravo Echo Tango: Oh yeah! I know it sounds strange, but it has always been a turn-on for me...just never found anyone for the job. LOL.

Chi-town Cutie: So what kind of stuff does he make you do?

Bravo Echo Tango: Flynn doesn't "make" me do anything. Everything he tells me to do, I want to do. It only looks like he is in control. I have all the power, really.

Flynn paused for a moment in consideration. *Is that how she sees me... as a puppet who is fooled into thinking that I am acting on my own, while the whole time she is secretly pulling my strings? She did hold a great deal of the power, and they both knew it...but all of the power?* Now he felt like the one that was submissive, playacting just for her benefit. The thought was emasculating. He could almost feel his penis shrink in shame.

Chi-town Cutie: If you say so. But my mom used to tell me every time I thought I had a man whipped, "Delores," (she used to call me Delores when she was scolding me, don't ask me why), "Someday you are going to run into a man that you can't wrap around your finger!"

Bravo Echo Tango: Wait! She did NOT say that! Didi, just the other day I heard a woman's voice saying, "This is not a man you can wrap around your finger, Delores. OMG, I can't believe what you just told me. Do you think it was your mother talking to me?

Chi-town Cutie: It sure sounds like it could have been. BTW, have you told your handsome hunk about your special "gift"?

Bravo Echo Tango: Not yet. I'm afraid to run him off, I guess. Believe me, this one I don't want to run off! Didi, I am really falling for him... hard.

This part Flynn could identify with. He kept strange secrets of his own. Besides, he was already acquainted with her "gift"…intimately.

Chi-town Cutie: Oh, Echo, please, please promise me you'll be careful!

Bravo Echo Tango: I will. I should get going. Flynn wants me to shower precisely at six…sounds like he has a big night planned.

Chi-town Cutie: Whatever you're into, I guess. Please be careful. I'll talk to you soon. Luv ya!

Bravo Echo Tango: Luv ya back! And don't worry, I have things under control.

Flynn re-read the last line. I have things under control. It felt like a direct hit to his male ego…these two women chit-chatting about him, and Echo bragging that she basically had him pussy whipped. Well maybe she did and maybe she didn't. Perhaps it was time to put his balls into this and find out who the real Master was in their relationship!

Unleashing the Animal Within

The sharp jangle of the telephone jolted Echo from her reverie. She placed her hand to her heart with a gasp.

"Oh, shit, that scared me!" she panted out loud.

Echo placed the phone to her ear. "Hel…"

"I'm dying to see you, sweetie," Flynn's familiar voice purred from the receiver. Echo's face brightened. He had left so abruptly, without as much as a kiss goodbye. "You are?"

"I have a little gift for you."

"You do? What is it?" Echo greedily fantasized about what type of gift he had bought for her.

"Don't ask or you won't get your present," interrupted Flynn. "Now be a good girl, and come to my place tonight at nine sharp. Don't be late, lass."

She had never been invited to Flynn's house before. She had assumed that he was a bachelor and that his house was probably in a constant state of disarray. For all she knew, he slept on a futon under a moth-eaten army blanket. Echo didn't know if she was looking forward to seeing him as much as she was looking forward to getting a glimpse of his house.

"Nine? That's good. I can be there." She confirmed.

"I'll be waiting. Don't be late. Oh, be sure and take a nice hot shower and a nap. I want you rested and fresh."

Before she could reply, the sound of a dial tone buzzed in her ear. Flynn was perhaps the most spontaneous person she had ever encountered. Everything happened on the spur of the moment with him, or so it seemed. Could it all just be a calculated effort to keep her off guard? Whatever it was, he was clearly in the driver's seat and she was along for the ride.

* * *

Echo groggily lifted her head from the couch cushion. Darkness surrounded her. *What time is it?* She wondered lazily. She knew it was past eight because she could see the moon suspended high in the night sky. Then she remembered that she was supposed to be at Flynn's house at nine. She turned on the lamp to look at her watch.

"Shit! Shit! Shit! Shit! Shit! Shit! Shit!" She cried, jumping off the couch and scurrying up the stairs to her bedroom. "Oh, damn it I'm late! He said nine, freaking nine, and now I've slept until nine twenty!"

Echo slipped on her shoes, brushed her teeth, tamed her wild hair and dashed down the street.

Standing nervously on the open porch, trying to catch her breath, she pressed her finger to the doorbell. The door flew open; Flynn appeared larger than life, filling the space of the doorframe. He reminded her of her father who used to wait up for the sound of her car crunching up the driveway when she was a teenager.

"You're late," he said plainly.

Echo slid past him into the foyer. The tone of his voice caused her stomach to bottom out with guilt. She secretly wished that she could shrink herself to size of a mouse, so that she could scuttle past him unnoticed.

Echo tried to act nonchalant. She surveyed his house for the first time. The rooms that she could view from the foyer were brimming with fine antiques and luxurious furnishings. Not a single item appeared out of place. *Very nice digs for a bachelor,* she thought.

She felt his stare shooting daggers into her back. She had better offer an explanation for her tardiness.

"I'm sorry I'm late. I overslept and I rushed right over as soon as I realized what time it was."

"Liar" Flynn retorted. "You took time to put on your shoes and brush your teeth and check your hair before you came over. I don't like a liar and I am not fond of being kept waiting."

Echo's mouth dropped open in astonishment. She couldn't believe her ears. "What did you just say? I know you didn't just call me a liar." Flynn raised his eyebrows in a challenging expression, as if to indicate "if the shoe fits…"

Why was he calling her names, and why was he so pissed off? And how did he know…

"How did you…never mind. I said I was sorry." She reached a

finger to stroke his cheek, but then thought better of it. His expression remained unflinchingly stern. She had been so excited to see him again… had thought about him every minute of the day. His displeasure stung and, as much as her knee-jerk reaction was to tell him to go fuck himself, she knew that she really didn't mean it. How would she have felt if the shoe was on the other foot? If he had kept her waiting, without so much as a phone call, she would have probably called him a selfish inconsiderate cocksucker. She dropped her eyes in thought and as she did, she spied the distinct bulge of an erection beneath his trousers.

Then it dawned on her—he was playing a game. *Alright*, she thought, *I'll submit.*

"I'm afraid that your tardiness has earned you a stern punishment." Flynn's thick brogue rolled from his mouth like honey.

"A punishment?" Echo wasn't certain that she liked the sound of that.

"Now, lass," his voice softer now, "what should the appropriate chastisement be for a naughty girl such as yourself?"

The first thought to enter Echo's head was, *I can think of a few things that might be fun. Like why don't you force me go down on you?* But she bit her tongue and held back the sharp comment. Instead she just batted her eyes and shrugged her shoulders.

Flynn began to slowly circle Echo as he had done the night before, stalking her. He paced menacingly round her, his hand gliding along her waist.

"I had been thinking on that exact subject when the doorbell rang. In fact, I had been thinking on that exact subject for twenty-seven full minutes. And here's how I decided that we shall proceed."

Echo didn't want to be reprimanded for looking at him, so she lowered her gaze to the floor, watching his shoes stop directly in front of her. "Since," he paused, "this is not your first infraction, I think a brisk …." Cupping her chin, Flynn leered at her with a look of conviction. "… spanking will do."

Flynn observed the startled expression on Echo's face. *Ah-ha! Gotcha!* He rejoiced. *We'll see what your friend in Chicago thinks of that!*

"A…what…a spanking?" Echo sputtered. "Even my parents never spanked me!"

"Perhaps they should have." He replied coolly. "You continue to defy me at every turn, Echo. You signed on for this, and it's a system of reward and punishment."

"But a spanking? Can't you just sit me in the corner or something?" Echo gestured wildly and stomped her feet. "Or how about detention? Have me write 'I will not be tardy' a hundred times."

She was trying to negotiate with him. Flynn was having none of it.

"Again, Echo, you'll just have to learn to trust me." Flynn persisted. "I promise you will like it far better than twenty minutes in time-out."

Like it? Echo had never thought about the possibility of liking it. She remembered seeing images of women dressed in black fishnet stockings and impossibly high stiletto pumps bent over a man's knee being spanked. The photos had titillated her. The women in the photos looked like they were enjoying themselves—just a harmless bit of sex play. "Okay," she acquiesced, "but not too hard."

"Good, it's decided, then." Flynn swept Echo into his arms, flinging her over his shoulder. He bounded up the staircase, Echo gripping onto his belt so she wouldn't slide off of his shoulder. The whole way up the stairs, Flynn rambled on. Echo wasn't certain if he was talking to her or just thinking out loud.

"No sense in wasting any more time. Let's get on with it. And don't think that you will be getting out of your punishment with a wink and a shake of that firm ass of yours, because you won't. I am disappointed with you, bloody damned disappointed. This is for your own good. I promise that it will hurt you more than it hurts me." Flynn kicked open the bedroom door and set Echo on her feet. Images of Bogart and Hemingway and warm nights in exotic places flooded Echo's imagination. The bedroom gleamed with polished woods. Carved mahogany posts soared over a massive bed covered in thick layers of sensuous linens. The earthy aroma of sandalwood enveloped the room. A single low stool sat in front of the fireplace.

Flynn gripped her upper arm, pulling her towards the stool. Placing pressure on her shoulders, he shoved her downward. Echo felt a jolt travel up her spine as her bottom hit the unforgiving surface.

Flynn towered above her. At that moment, he was the sexiest man Echo had ever laid eyes on. Flynn possessed the rare physique that comes to a man naturally. He was not bulging with the over-built, iron-pumping brand of muscle. His body was lean and hard and perfectly proportioned. The muscles of his chest were rippling with tension beneath his white silk shirt. The disobedient lock of hair dangled over his right eye. Echo shivered with excitement at the sight of him looming powerfully over her. She thrilled to his new dynamic dominance.

A scowl crossed his face. Perhaps this wasn't a game. He actually looked pissed off. She had disappointed him. She hadn't meant to, but the mistake had been hers. At first she was incredulous that Flynn would be so upset because she had been a bit tardy. But now, she began to see it from his perspective. He had been waiting for her. He must have thought she wasn't going to show or that she was purposely defying him. She reminded herself to be careful not to inflame his displeasure further.

Reaching into his pocket, Flynn walked behind her. Something was placed over her eyes, blocking her vision. Echo brought her fingers to her face and felt a wide satin band covering her eyes. Echo's head jerked back slightly as she felt a tightening in her scalp. She could no longer sense, nor hear Flynn. She turned her head right and left trying to locate him, sniffing the air for his scent and listening intently for the smallest sound that would indicate his location.

"Open your mouth."

Echo jumped backward. Flynn's voice came from in front of her. She parted her lips, unsure whether he was going to kiss her or place a gag in her mouth. Unexpectedly she tasted the flavor of sweet, red wine. It spilled from her lips and coursed down her neck.

"Now look at what's happened. Your pretty blouse is all ruined." Flynn admonished. "We'll just have to get rid of it."

The blouse was ripped from Echo's body. She heard the sound of buttons popping off and hitting the floor. Her skin prickled in the cold air. She felt his hand encircle her neck, and then slowly his fingernails dragged down her breast bone, and over her stomach. Her breathing came faster as her muscles twitched in response to his touch.

"Might as well get rid of these too," said Flynn, pulling her legs up by the feet and shaking her pants down her legs. Echo's fingers gripped the stool to keep from falling off.

"You can keep your shoes on."

Dressed now in only black pumps and red thong panties, Echo shivered. A swift boot from behind propelled the stool, with Echo on it, rolling across the floor. Her stomach lurched and she braced herself for an impact. But the stool slowed and spun to a stop. She felt a source of heat on her face and breasts. A pop and a hiss and the aroma of burning logs told her that she was within a foot or so from the fireplace.

"Stand up," Flynn commanded.

Flynn slipped behind her and lowered himself onto the stool. He clutched Echo's waist, brusquely pulling her onto his lap. Her bare bottom made a slapping sound against his thigh. He wasn't going to address the issue of the instant message conversation. He wanted to save that for another, more rational time.

"Are you sorry that you kept me waiting for twenty-seven minutes?"

Echo nodded affirmatively.

"Ah—ah—ah! It is 'yes, sir, I am sorry'. Say it."

"Yes sir, I am sorry."

She quivered. He needed to reassure her that she was in no real danger, yet maintain his dominance.

"I hope you are telling the truth." He cupped her breast in his hand, feeling the firm weight of it in his palm. He traced his thumb over her pink bud, exciting it to attention. Her lips parted and he felt her relax.

Flynn lowered his voice. "First, I am going to explain the rules of this game. Keep in mind that no matter how real it feels, it is just a game that can be called off at any time."

Echo turned her ear attentively toward Flynn's voice.

"I don't see any sense in thinking up some exotic word when 'Uncle' will do. It's simple and you won't forget it. Just like when you were a child, if there is anything that you don't go along with, all you have to say is, 'Uncle'. Just say 'Uncle' and I'll know to stop, alright?"

Flynn noticed Echo begin to nod her head. He squeezed her breast as a reminder.

"Yes, sir, I understand," she remembered.

Good, she was learning.

"There may be times when you won't be able to speak, or to gesture. In that case, shake your head from side to side. If I don't hear 'Uncle' or see you shake your head, I'll assume that you are fine with whatever is happening."

Tonight would be a test of her trust. Would she go all the way or back out? Either way, Flynn had to find out.

"If you're ready, let's begin." "I'm ready." She gulped. In a single swift movement Flynn clutched Echo by the arm and flung her over his knee. "What a ripe, round bottom you have. Let's see if we can make it rosy as well." Flynn rubbed his hand in firm circles on Echo's buttocks.

His palm connected with her flesh. Her body jumped. Her buttocks stung and she felt a creeping heat beneath her skin. The sudden pain was followed by a pleasurable emotion. It was a scandalous discovery. Flynn was reminding her that she was a bad girl—a very bad girl. She wanted Flynn to spank the bad right out of her.

"What a naughty girl you are," he teased. "Wicked too….don't forget wicked. You are an exceedingly wicked girl."

Echo moaned. Wicked, yes, she was a wicked, naughty girl who did terrible things.

"Are you enjoying this?" Flynn asked. "Let me see."

Flynn stuck his fingers beneath her panties and stroked her pussy.

Echo was slick with arousal. He searched for her clit and found it erect, the tiny tip jumping beneath his finger. She was responding perfectly.

As he explored her wet willingness, his cock awakened. Flynn saw the impression of his fingers on her plump cheek, a glowing reminder of the swat he had landed. He pushed her further into her submission.

"You wayward, warped little girl! You clearly are taking a great deal of delight in your punishment. "Would you like another whack?"

Echo craved another spanking. The burn of his hand, like a sudden loud noise in the middle of the night, sparked her senses. Flynn's taunts about what a wicked girl she was made her want to act hopelessly incorrigible.

"Y-yes, sir, I deserve another!"

"Sorry, no more for now. "

No more? How disappointing. Now he was punishing her for enjoying her punishment. Dammit, just when she was getting aroused. She lay across his knees, waiting for a movement from him; when none came forth she started to remove herself from Flynn's lap.

Another burning slap connected with her backside.

"Ouch!" she screamed. *That one smarted.*

"I didn't say that you could stand. I make the rules here, lass, not you."

She had blundered again. But at least he had given her another stimulating spank. Now the skin on her buttocks tingled. Flynn rubbed the burn away with the flat of his palm. The sting diminished.

"Who is your Master?"

Echo knew the answer that he was expecting. She momentarily considered giving the wrong response, betting that he would spank her again, but that was not a wager she was willing to make.

"You are!" she cried out.

"Correct. And I suggest you don't forget it."

Echo braced herself for another blow. Flynn's palm methodically circled her buttocks. His hand was a cool balm against her burning flesh. "To whom do you give your power?"

At this moment Echo didn't feel as if she had much power to give. She was in Flynn's home, stretched nearly naked across his knees and blindfolded. What additional power could she possibly give him? His dominance tonight was unflinching. "To you…to you," she answered.

Echo jumped as her ass blazed with yet another punishing strike which ignited her passion anew. She hadn't answered the question with much conviction and he had sensed it. She was being a bad and willful girl again. She had grown into an undisciplined woman, and like an errant child she secretly craved boundaries but at the same time reveled in her misbehavior.

"You hesitated," Flynn reproached. "Are you wavering Echo? Do you not want me to have your power? If you don't want me to, then just say so."

"I…I give my power to you, Master." Echo's bottom felt as if it was scorched. She no longer wanted another spanking.

Suddenly, Echo's body was lifted into the air. With deliberate strides, Flynn carried her across the room. Echo felt herself tip as her feet found the floor. The firm wood of a bed pillar pressed into her back. Grasping her left hand and then her right, Flynn pulled them both behind her waist and around the pillar. Circles of cold steel imprisoned her wrists. The metal tightened and the cuffs ratcheted shut with an ominous click.

Echo wriggled her wrists, settling them into a comfortable position. Flynn's breath was on her neck, hot and urgent. His lips moved up her throat, then covered her ear. She yielded to his mouth. The moist, silkiness of his tongue in her ear contrasted sharply with the ache that burned her punished bottom.

Flynn whispered in her ear, his breath blowing fine strands of hair onto her face. "You're an impish, disobedient woman and you make my blood rise. I want you to demonstrate just how wicked you can be."

Wicked, yes wicked—make me do wickedly bad things.

She recognized the feeling of Flynn's erection pressing against her stomach. His hands caressed her breasts. He groaned. The sound of his pleasure excited Echo, making her juices spread through the fabric of her panties, wetting her thighs.

"Present yourself to me in the kneeling position."

Flynn's hands applied pressure to Echo's shoulder. Where was he going with this?

She had no way of knowing. She worked her imprisoned arms down the pillar, carefully finding the floor with her knees. There was only silence now. The only sound Echo heard was the thumping of her own heart reverberating in her ears. After many moments the clatter of a belt buckle broke the stillness. The rip of a metal zipper sounded closely near her right ear and she heard the zipper catch a bit. She imagined that Flynn needed to maneuver it over his erection. When she turned her head in the direction of the sound, Flynn's cock brushed her lips. It pushed against her mouth as if to say, "Let me in."

"Remember when you wanted to suck my big, fat cock? You begged for it. Now show me what a wicked tart you are, and suck my prick."

Parting her lips, Echo received Flynn's cock into her mouth. It was magnificent; extensive, broad and hard enough to cut a diamond. The skin was stretched tightly across the silky, driving head. The girth of his shaft filled the whole of her hungry mouth.

A low growl escaped from Flynn's throat. With agonizing precision, Echo worked his cock in and out of her mouth. She wanted to cup his balls and feel their firm weight in her palm, but her hands remained trapped in the restraints.

Flynn stroked her hair and, giving it a painful jerk backwards, began fucking her mouth. His hips gyrated with each thrust of his rigid prick causing his cock to swirl over her palate and tongue. Drops of saliva fell from her lips and drizzled down her breasts. She tipped her head back slightly to take his full length into her mouth. His hair tickled her nose as he sunk his shaft deep into her throat. Swallowing, she relaxed her throat muscles to accommodate his mammoth crank.

Echo loved giving oral gratification. She'd been told it was her enjoyment of the act that made her so good at it. She ministered to his prick with worshipful gulps. She wished that she had her hands available so she could use them to increase his pleasure. But she did her best with her mouth and tongue, savoring every delectable inch of his iron rod.

Flynn slowed his thrusting, pulling his javelin from her lips and then easing its length back into her mouth. He growled with rapture.

"That's my naughty girl," he gasped. "You know what I like, don't you?"

Knowing that she was pleasing him incited a flame inside of Echo. Her basest instincts stirred and bubbled to the surface. She became feral and untamed; a tigress devouring her prey.

Flynn's loins tightened in response to Echo's skillful mouth. He had to slow things down or he was going to blow. She was clearly immersed in the act and he was being swept up in her unchecked passion.

Flynn withdrew his cock from her grasping lips, leaving Echo's mouth open in supplication. She squirmed, adjusting her restrained arms. Still her mouth sought his penis.

He taunted her lips with the engorged head of his rod. When her tongue reached to taste it, she would find that it was just beyond her reach.

"You are such a dreadful girl!" he panted. "What am I going to do with you?"

Her beckoning mouth was too big a temptation. Flynn held his prick in his hand pressing it to her moist lips. Echo's pink tongue lashed at the purple head, her lips pursed around the tip, applying a gentle sucking pressure.

Flynn closed his eyes and stroked his turgid shaft with his hand. Her mouth was as scorching as a Mexican summer and twice as humid. He feared that if rammed his length into its sultry temptation again that he would blow his white-hot wad down her throat and send her on a psychic trip that she wasn't expecting.

Echo knew by the increasing rigidity of his cock that Flynn was nearing the edge. Her arms began to burn, and she shifted uncomfortably as she slowed her oral stimulation of his glans. Any other time, she would have gladly taken him to climax with her mouth, but tonight, she wanted him in her pussy. She didn't want to give him any reason not to fuck her. So, her mouth urged him to the brink and not a centimeter farther.

The ache in her arms worsened. She wiggled them and shifted her weight, trying to release the pressure.

"Are you in pain, lass?" His voice held a trace of panic and guilt.

"Just a little, sir," Echo replied. She didn't want to appear wimpy, but her shoulders and neck were getting sore.

Immediate relief eased into the muscles of her arms as Flynn lifted her onto her feet.

"Here now, stand up. Are you alright?" Flynn probed.

Echo stretched her back and arms. The tension was gone. "I'm fine now, thank you." Echo's voice was little more than a whisper.

Flynn placed his mouth on hers, opening her lips with his tongue. Something small and tasting bitterly metallic slipped past her teeth. Flynn pulled his mouth from hers. Examining the object with her teeth and tongue, she determined that it was a tiny key.

"I seem to be all out of pockets," said Flynn. "Be a good lass and hold that for me, please. Try not to swallow it. I believe you are going to want it later."

Then she knew—it was the key to the handcuffs. If she swallowed it, she would remain imprisoned on the post until...well, until. She tucked the key behind her bottom lip with her tongue, and pressed her lips together tightly to keep it from escaping.

This was what Flynn meant earlier about her not being able to speak the safe word. So far, she hadn't the slightest inclination to utter it, and now she couldn't.

The strap of her thong cut sharply into her hips, followed by a ripping sound. Echo nearly cried out, but remembered the key. Cool air wafted across her over-heated pussy, which had been kept warm and damp by her panties. She was entirely naked now.

Just when she thought that she could read and predict his actions, he changed like a chameleon; alternating between the extremes of pain and pleasure, fear and comfort, and back again. Echo began to expect the unexpected. She was learning more than just an understanding of the extremes; she was eagerly anticipating, and relishing in her response to them.

A hand reached between her trembling thighs, tickling the curly hairs and placing her on alert. Fingers moved along her dewy folds, then entered her throbbing pussy. She welcomed their intrusion by tightening her muscles around them, sucking them farther into her depths. Flynn played her like a well-loved instrument and her body sang forth with a sensual tune, each touch releasing a new and glorious note.

His torrid breath heated her flesh and the fevered moistness of his mouth engulfed her right breast. It was heavenly. He suckled her tit and she undulated to his touch. Each lick and nibble drove her craving closer to the surface. In her mind she wailed, *fuck me, Flynn. Fuck me hard and long.*

He bit her nipple sharply as his hands reached behind her hips. Echo's feet left the ground as Flynn's hand supported her weight. His cock pushed against her slick opening and plunged into her pink pit of pleasure, nearly toppling her backward.

Flynn's strong arm caught her. She quickly lifted her legs and cinched them around his waist, clamping herself tightly to him.

At last she possessed him. His prick was trapped deep inside of her pussy prison and she wasn't about to release it.

Flynn gripped her buttocks, his nails scratching her skin. She was suspended in mid-air, her arms bound behind her and her legs clutching his hips. The only thing keeping her from falling was his powerful prick spearing her to the bedpost. She braced herself for a good, hard drilling. *Come on baby, show me who's the boss.*

Flynn held her hips and thrust his shaft into her. Her ravenous vice of love contracted on his prick. Throwing his head back, a long groan of pleasure croaked from his throat. If she had wanted this, he had wanted it more.

Echo's breasts bounced to and fro as he bucked into her. He yearned to squeeze them in his hands and roll her tempting pink nubs between his fingers, but his hands needed to support her weight, so all he could do was watch her spectacular tits bouncing in rhythm with his thrusting, shaking and jiggling with the earthquake of his pounding. She was so fucking beautiful. He wanted to give her a screwing that she would never forget as long as she lived—even if she lived forever.

The slap-slapping of their pelvises rang in his ears. The harder he hammered her, the more ferociously she clung to him. Her jaw was clenched tightly and Flynn could see the muscles of her neck, tense and throbbing.

He was ramming her like a freight train, relishing the scorching heat of her cunt; he had to slow himself down. His lungs heaving and sweat seeping from his pores, Flynn took a moment to gather his senses. He withdrew his cock until just the head was still inside of her quivering slit. Echo squirmed and quaked, demanding the full length of his battering ram. Flynn teased her by gently pulsing his cock head in and out of her opening. She squeezed him with her legs, trying to force him into her, but Flynn resisted the tempting offer a few moments longer. He wanted to savor the joy of entering and re-entering her over and over again.

Echo moaned and writhed. Flynn stilled his movements, trying to regain her focus. She seemed to have become lost in passion, squirming and panting like an animal in heat. He wanted to still her feral cravings, coax her back from the brink so she could really experience what was happening. He withdrew his prick, and slowly stroked her ass with his hands.

"That's right, baby," he soothed. "Don't be in such a hurry."

Finally, her legs no longer tried to compel him into her. She was relaxing into the moment. Just when she had melted into a quiet state of bliss, Flynn rammed his prick into her, grinding his hips in a circular motion against her clit.

"Who's your Master, now?" he grunted, his balls drawing tightly into his groin. Echo's head dropped backward between her outstretched arms, her hair skimming the floor. A tell-tale red flush blossomed on her breasts. Her abdomen muscles fluttered and twitched. Flynn held her onto his prick, cradling her body in his arms as he drew his rod from her in slow increments and then invaded her once again. Echo writhed and grunted like a wild beast. Her legs imprisoned his torso and her undulating cunt tortured his cock.

His fingers tightened on her flesh as her cunt throbbed and strangled his cock with the forceful, rapid contractions of her orgasm.

The pressure in his prick grew more urgent as she milked him to climax. He quickly extracted his pulsing phallus from her bruised lips. His balls pulled tightly against his groin. His body trembled from the volcano of cum that coursed its way up his engorged shaft. The agonizing intensity of release caused an unearthly howl to bellow forth from his throat as his red-hot load splashed over her neck and breasts, its glistening drops spattering on her pale flesh.

Her body went limp and her legs hung loosely from her hips. Flynn deftly caught her weight in his arms, supporting her so that she did not crash to the floor.

She was eerily quiet. All the color had drained from her face. Flynn patted her cheek, but she was unresponsive. His chest seized, and his pulse quickened. Something was wrong. Had he pulled out too late and sent her soaring out of her body? He reached to remove the handcuffs and then he remembered. The key! *Sweet Jaysus, had she choked?* His panicked heart pounded as his finger searched her mouth. With a sigh of relief, he felt the key tucked behind her lip. She was breathing heavily, but making no other movement. Flynn carefully but swiftly lowered her to the ground and freed her wrists.

"Echo, Echo, Jaysus, girl, please wake up," he called, trying to rouse her.

Flynn pushed the blindfold above her eyes. Echo blinked, her green eyes adjusting to the light. Someone was calling her name. For a moment she glimpsed Flynn's face. He looked terrified. She couldn't imagine what he might be so afraid of. She felt better than she ever had in her entire life. She managed a smile, closed her eyes and the darkness claimed her once more.

* * *

Echo awoke wrapped in Flynn's secure embrace. The first light of day had not yet broken through the blue-black sky. She spooned nearer to him, snuggling into the billowy featherbed. His arms tightened around her, offering the joy of skin on skin.

"It's still early, lass. Return to dreamland if you want."

"Mmmm, "she mumbled, "it's cold in here."

Flynn held her tighter still and pulled a scarlet coverlet over her shoulder.

"Better?"

"Much...Flynn, are you still angry with me for being late?"

Flynn thought back. His anger was a dim memory. He had lain awake all night, petrified that he had hurt her.

"Ah, lass, you needed some discipline. It's sometimes my heartbreaking role to provide that for you. I was never really all that angry with you. How can I stay angry with mo chuisle?"

"Muh-what?"

"Mo chuisle. Say it after me. Muh... kwish...la." He pronounced the word from deep in his throat.

"Muh...kwish...la?" she repeated.

"It means, 'my pulse'. Haven't you guessed it? You are my pulse."

His pulse...what did that mean? A pulse pumps blood. Blood is the substance that keeps creatures alive. Was he trying to say that she was his reason for living?

Tears welled up in Echo's eyes. "Flynn, that is the most beautiful thing that anyone has ever said to me." "It is truer than you know. My heart beats because of you. Rest awhile now, mo chuisle." Echo turned the phrase over and over in her mind like a lullaby...mo chuisle....mo chuisle...mo chuisle.

A Cold Wind

The sound of running water roused Echo from her slumber. She pushed herself up, sitting against the massive headboard, rubbing her eyes. No sign of the previous night's activities remained. Her clothing and shoes were gone. At the foot of the bed perched a satin box topped with a white bow. Echo removed the lid and lifted out a flowing dressing gown made of fine Irish lace. A note card fell from the folds of the gown. Your bath is waiting. xxxx Flynn.

Was he for real? Echo laid her head on the pillow where Flynn had slept. His scent lingered on the linens and she filled her lungs with the aroma until it swam in her head. She tried to piece together her memories of the night before. She wanted to capture each detail and impress it into her memory before it flitted away. The fierceness with which they had made love was more than lust—at least for her it was. She wanted to possess Flynn and to be possessed by him. She had never before felt so deeply connected to another person.

But how connected could they be? She hadn't shared her secret with him. She needed to do that, and soon. The thought filled her with terror. She knew it was the fear of losing him that had kept her quiet, yet she knew she couldn't allow much more time to pass before she spilled the beans. They were both wading in too deep waters. She would just have to find the right time.

Echo lifted her head from the pillow. She was a little woozy, as if she had drunk too much the night before. Funny, she couldn't really recall what happened after her orgasm. There was a moment, when he was buried deep inside of her, when she felt drenched in a sublime euphoria.

Echo squeezed her eyes tightly, trying to jar the memory loose. She wondered if it was a hallucination, but she distinctly remembered being out of her body, floating above herself, connected by a long silvery rope which emerged from her navel. Flashes of green, the sounds of their lovemaking in the distance, a weightless, peaceful feeling, like a dream she couldn't quite recall, but that haunted her long after she had awakened.

Whatever had occurred, Echo felt electrified and energetic this morning. A nice hot bath sounded very appealing.

Shaking off the images that shadowed her mind, she slid her legs off the side of the bed and skipped towards the sound of running water. A shiny, brass door handle in the shape of a swan announced the entrance to the bath. Echo stepped into the room. Tiny soap bubbles rose from a cavernous soaking tub, and then disappeared into the perfumed air. A steamy waterfall gushed from a silver spout. Echo spied a covered serving tray and a single white rose placed near the tub. Passing by a gilt-framed mirror, she caught a glimpse of herself. Her hair was wild like a lioness, and her face was aglow. Blushing, Echo lowered herself into the warm suds.

"Well lass, you look like you have been rode hard and put away wet." said Flynn, shaking his head and clucking as he entered the room.

"Don't let me stop you from enjoying your breakfast. Go on girl; dig in before all of my culinary efforts grow cold and tasteless." Flynn moved the tray toward her and whisked the gleaming dome from it.

"Blueberry pancakes! My favorite! How did you know?" Echo exclaimed. Not waiting for his answer, she dove into the sticky stack of pancakes.

"MMMM...isth goot," mumbled Echo, giving Flynn the 'thumbs up' sign.

"Do you like the gift?"

"Oh, yes, Flynn," Echo replied, shoveling forkfuls of pancakes into her mouth. "I love it, I really do."

"Good, I'm glad." Flynn knelt down beside the bathtub, turning off the faucet.

Echo laid her fork down with finality, and wiped her mouth with a white linen napkin, placing the tray on the floor beside the tub.

Flynn dipped a large sea sponge into the water. He held the sodden sponge above her back, soothing droplets cascaded down her spine.

No one had ever pampered her like this before. She felt truly loved and protected.

Flynn sat on a small bench near the tub, wearing only his striped pajama bottoms. He had become very quiet. He dripped scented oil in the center of the sponge. The scent of lemongrass and citrus wafted through the air. Echo, feeling tranquil and full of blueberry pancakes, slid deeper into the water, closing her eyes.

Flynn loved to watch her enjoyment. It gave him tremendous pleasure to make her happy. He picked up her arm, her hand hung languidly from her wrist. Soapy rivulets coursed their way down her skin. He massaged the silky sponge over each of her fingers, down her arm and over her breast.

For a moment last night, he was terrified that he had lost her. He needed to be more careful. He'd better wear a condom until…

"Why don't you join me?" Echo interrupted his reverie.

"Would you like that?" Flynn asked.

"I think it would be grand, just grand." Echo giggled trying to imitate Flynn's accent.

Flynn took the imitation as flattery and beamed at her. She was cute as a bug this morning and in a wonderful, playful mood. This might be a good time to confess what he had been yearning to tell her. It was a manipulation, he knew, but if he could put her on the defensive…coax her to confess her on-line indiscretion, which he would generously forgive, then perhaps opening those lines of communication could open the door for him to reveal his secret. It was a gamble, but worth a try.

Flynn undressed and eased into the water behind her, his legs wrapping around her narrow hips. Her thin frame looked so tiny next to his, with her pale, smooth skin contrasting against the dark hairs of his muscled legs. She was all undulating curves, while he was hard surfaces and sharp angles. She was the most beautiful creature his eyes had ever beheld.

Echo scooted forward, leaning her head back to rest on his chest. It was a small thing, but it warmed Flynn to the core. It communicated that she was in his care, bonding to him in more than a sexual way.

Flynn wrapped his arms around her chest, his hands on her shoulders, and held her snugly against his body. They fitted together like two pieces of a puzzle. He kissed the top of her head and squeezed her more tightly. It was as if he couldn't be close enough to her.

He knew that he was spoiling her, but he couldn't help himself. She was a woman that was born to be spoiled. She was so soft and feminine, but with a fire that burned so fiercely it had scorched lesser men than him. Flynn pushed her shoulders down until her head was floating in the water. Her hair drifted like a million strands of shimmering silk upon the surface, reminding him of a sunset over Loughrea Lake.

Flynn tipped her chin back with his hand and brought her up from the water. Filling his palms with shampoo, he washed the suds into her hair. She appeared at ease and, Flynn hoped, receptive. He decided to take the first tentative steps.

"Echo," he began, "Have you told anyone about us…about me?"

Echo became very quiet. Why was she hesitating?

"What do you mean?" she hedged.

"Just wondering…have you mentioned or talked about me to anyone?"

Flynn dipped her head back into the water and rinsed the soap from her hair. She was stalling for time; he could feel it. He wasn't trying to be tricky. He wanted to give her a chance to tell him on her own. He didn't want to thrust the evidence in her face and rain accusations down upon her.

"No," she answered. "I haven't told anyone."

"No-one? You're certain?"

Echo reached her hand behind her back and stroked his cock. "I don't want to talk right now, Flynn. Let's make love instead."

She was playing him, using her feminine wiles to distract him, again. This wasn't going as planned. He had an agenda, and she was throwing him off. If she would just admit what she had done, it would be simpler. In his mind he had the scene worked out. He could tell her that's it's okay and he really isn't all that upset. She would be so grateful for his understanding that when he admitted to having a confession of his own, she might not be so quick to pass judgment and would listen quietly and give him a chance to explain.

"Not now, Echo. I don't feel like it. I'd really like to talk about something with you."

"I bet I can make you feel like it." She turned around, rubbing her wet breasts against him.

Flynn turned his head from her advances. His frustration at the way she used sex to distract him started to seethe in his chest. He had given her the opportunity to be honest with him, but she was clearly doing everything she could to avoid it. "Come on, Echo. Not right now."

She stroked her soapy hands along the length of his prick. It swelled and grew turgid despite his protestations.

"See, you do want to fuck."

"Echo, no...can't we just talk for a while? There are some things I want to discuss with you." Flynn tried to push her hands away, but she only gripped him more tightly, a hungry look in her eyes.

"Fuck me Flynn—right here, right now. Fuck me." She breathed.

Normally he wouldn't be insulted at an invitation for a healthy fuck, but something in the way she used it to manipulate him gripped at his heart. It made him think she didn't respect him as a person, and it made him feel like nothing more than a stud service. Was that all he was to her—a good fuck? He must have misread her signals. When she told him that she loved him that night in the hotel room, what had she meant... that she loved his mouth, his cock, his flesh, but not him?

He thought of the instant messages he had read...she was in control... she was the one with all the power. He remembered the words she had spoken to him on her sofa. Fuck 'em and forget 'em. A sad realization dawned on him. He was nothing but a boy-toy to her... something to brag about to her girlfriends. He had given everything to her and was prepared to give more. He had played her game, indulged her fantasy, and wracked his brain to figure out what made her happy and what didn't.

Had she ever asked, even once, what she could do for him? Seeing his plan dissipate was frustrating, but the sense that he was being used was even more deflating.

He willingly performed the role of her Master, but he would not be her whore!

"Fuck you? You want me to fuck you? I clothe you. I feed you, I wash you, and I bend to your will much too often for your own good. I even deny myself my own pleasure to increase yours, and now *you* tell *me* when and where to fuck you!" Flynn sputtered, rising out of the bathtub. Wrapping a towel around his waist, he stood in front of Echo, his prick poking out from the folds.

He could feel the blood rising in his veins and he knew he was rocketing towards an emotional explosion, but he was helpless to curtail it. A lethal mixture of humiliation, frustration and anger boiled in his being. He felt it ascending from his core, blasting through his chest, and the words spewed from his mouth.

"Is this what you want?" He held his cock with one hand and taunted her with it. "Where do you want my big prick today, you wicked tart;

jammed down your gullet, drilling your pussy till you scream; or would you prefer I stick it up your tight little ass?"

Echo's eyes grew wide, the color draining from her cheeks. He saw her shock, but had little sympathy for her at this moment. He wanted her to feel half the hurt he was feeling. This woman, this mortal, thought she could play with him, use him and abuse him. He had been nothing but generous with her and yet she hadn't given him the courtesy of a conversation since the first moment he had awakened her sexual beast. From the start, she had gotten what she wanted and his needs be damned.

Flynn's hand stroked his shaft. "I suppose you also want me to lick your cunt as well, you unappreciative girl!"

"Stop it Flynn," she begged, slapping the water with her hands.

Flynn's hand flew faster over his penis, his fury building to a crescendo. "Now that you have me in your bed, I suppose I'm not good enough to talk to, or be honest with. I'm just a hard cock and an open wallet to you."

"Uncle!" she cried, "Uncle! Uncle!"

"I thought I meant more to you than just a fuck buddy. I don't think you'll ever learn to trust me or to care about me as a person…" He gripped his prick, it spasmed in his hand as his seed splashed onto the remains of the blueberry pancakes.

"… and that's what I think of your 'fuck me Flynn'" The door shook violently as he slammed it behind him.

* * *

Echo angrily wrapped the dressing gown around her. "I knew this guy was too good to be true! What kind of fucked up shit was that? Stupid, stupid…how could I be so flipping stupid to think I had found Mr. Perfect?" muttered Echo, her eyes stinging with tears.

Sure, she had fibbed to him, but he didn't know that. She hadn't wanted to get into a big scene and spoil the mood of last night. Now the memory was sullied by his tirade. Her head began to spin and she choked back the sensation of nausea. Her thoughts wrapped round and round, forming a tangled mess in her mind. She couldn't think straight, and she was hyperventilating. She sat on the edge of the toilet putting her head between her legs, willing herself to get a grip.

She had to get out of this house. She couldn't bear to see him again right now. She wanted to go home and try to figure out what had just happened.

She walked to the door, put her ear against the crack and listened for any sounds of Flynn moving around in the bedroom. Hearing none, she opened the door, and was surprised to see Flynn dressed and standing before the fire. He looked so smug, so righteous, so back in control. The sight of his arrogance caused a fire of rage to burn hotly in her chest. Drops of perspiration sprung on the back of her neck.

"Where are my clothes? Where are my goddamn clothes, you sick son-of-a-bitch?" she sputtered. "I want to go home right now and I can't exactly walk down the street in this little number with my ass and tits on display!" Her voice rose. Fury filled her and she wanted to hurt him the way he had hurt her. "Speaking of homes, one of us is going to sell theirs, because I'm getting a restraining order that says you can't come within a thousand miles of me, you freak!"

Anger and pain clawed at her. Why had he talked to her like that, as if she was a sexual deviant and he wasn't a willing participant? She could kick herself for allowing this to happen. She had opened her heart and he had taken it, shredded it, and thrown it back at her in tatters.

Men had been nothing but fucking problems for her all her life and, right now, this man represented every rejection, every lie, every disappointment she had been dealt by every testosterone-wielding Neanderthal who had crossed her path. Echo had to clench her hands into tight little fists so she wouldn't claw his eyes out with her bare fingers.

"I don't know what I ever saw in you…you disgust me! It is so cliché, but it's true nonetheless. I want to tell you something, Mr. Irish Don Juan; I went along with all of your kinky little games. I enjoyed myself immensely. I freely admit. In fact, you held me spellbound; but that revolting bit of theatrics in there…that totally crossed the fucking line!"

"It was *you* who crossed the line." Flynn flung the typed pages in her direction. They fluttered to the floor at her feet.

"What?" Echo snapped, not understanding. Flynn's hand was on the door, his other hand pointing to the pages on the floor. "You, Echo, it was you." Flynn flung open the door, exited the room, and slammed the door behind him with such force that a large oil painting came crashing to the floor.

Echo gathered the papers from the floor. One glance told her what they contained. Tears of guilt and self-hatred sprang forth like blood from a wound. She had lied to him and he knew it.

She'd had a problem with telling white lies her whole life. It wasn't something she was proud of. Shame and regret prickled icily beneath her skin as she remembered her mother saying, "I swear, you would rather climb a tree and tell a lie than stand on the ground and tell the truth."

She didn't set out to lie, it just happened sometimes. Echo realized now how immature and hurtful it could be.

She tried to put herself in Flynn's place. A conversation, which she knew in the back of her mind he had asked her not to have, had seemed innocent enough to her. But when he'd read it, which he shouldn't have done…she could see how he might have thought she was turning him into a cuckold. When she lied, his suspicions were validated all the more.

Her skin crawled with shame and embarrassment. He had known about the conversation the whole time that he was questioning her. He had given her a chance to come clean. She had trusted him with her body, but not her secrets. She had fallen from his grace.

He had lashed out, and she had struck back. Both of them were so volatile it was chilling.

What could she have been thinking leaping into a dom/sub relationship with him? Maybe she wasn't cut out for this lifestyle at all. Their roles had always seemed muddled. It was a constant struggle for who was on top.

He was right about one thing. What had she done for him? Shouldn't she have been the one to order his breakfast and run his bath? She hadn't even thought to perform these small acts of affection for him. She was so grateful for his attentions that she had allowed him to pile them on her, sucking in his kindnesses like a leech.

A single tear slid across her lips to the corner of her mouth. Echo crumpled to the floor, sobbing her torment into her hands. The things he had said to her…the things she had said to him. She cringed just thinking about how the passion of the night before had turned so cruel. If only she could take it back. She had to explain, tell him that she was sorry, that she only lied because she was afraid of losing him.

She couldn't have come all this way just to watch him walk out the door. She had to talk to him, to try and pick up the pieces before it was too late.

"Flynn! Flynn!" she called, as she raced down the staircase, her lacy gown floating behind her. She searched through the maze of rooms looking for him until she came upon her clothes, folded neatly upon the kitchen table, buttons sewn and all. But Flynn was gone.

* * *

Back in the familiar surroundings of her home, day turned to night and night slipped back into day. Each moment was like a waking dream. Echo shopped. She ate a little and tried to write. She forced herself to go through the motions of being alive, but the world had lost its vibrancy. The last leaves that clung to the trees dried up and dropped to the ground, leaving naked branches rocking in the wind. The landscape turned harsh and gloomy. Even the sky mimicked her mood by shifting to a somber shade of grey. When a cold nor'easter wind blew in, Echo felt the chill cut straight through to her soul.

Everything reminded her of Flynn. One morning, a small flock of white birds flew high overhead. Looking up from the street, Echo thought that they looked like the X's that Flynn had signed on the card in the gift box. It was as if those kisses had turned into birds that had flown right out of her life. She was certain now that she loved Flynn, because it hurt so badly to lose him. Two weeks had passed without a single sign of him. She had deliberately walked past his house several times, hoping he would see her. But he didn't emerge. She wondered if he even lived there anymore.

The house was dark as pitch. She had left notes in his mailbox, but each time she deposited one, the others were still in the box. She listened for his voice or even the disembodied voice that sounded like his, but no message reached her ears. Even the spirits had abandoned her.

Echo was consumed with regret. The only man she had ever truly cared about had slipped through her fingers like dust in the wind—all over a stupid misunderstanding.

It was doubtful that she would ever know that kind of happiness again. Just like pain and pleasure, love had its polar opposite and it wasn't hate—it was despair.

Each day, Echo descended a step further back into her old life. By the time that she tallied day seventeen of Flynn's absence on her calendar, she was beginning to feel a tiny bit grateful for Flynn staying out of sight. She had never felt a loss so deeply, and she never, ever wanted to feel like this again. If he came back into her life, she would fall in love all over again, and then what? More torment?

She remembered the time when Flynn had quoted Kennedy to her.

Well, she was certainly Irish through and through, because the world broke her heart at every turn, and she was weary of it.

She reasoned that, if she never saw Flynn again, she would be able to gradually erase the memory and agony from her life. But reason couldn't cure the ache she felt in her heart.

As the weeks passed, Echo resigned herself to never seeing Flynn again. She finalized it in her mind. The affair was over; time to get on with the business of living.

Then on day twenty-one of their separation, Echo went to the library.

A Poet's Plea

"May I help you?" asked the paunchy, balding librarian.

"I hope so," said Echo sweetly. "I am looking for…"

"She is looking for a self-help book….I believe it's called 'I'm OK, You're a Sick Son-of-a Bitch'. Do you know if you have that in your catalog?"

Echo did not have to turn around to know who was standing behind her. Her heart leapt and sank in one swift motion.

"Never mind," she said to the bewildered librarian.

"You know what, lad; I believe that I can assist her in finding exactly what she is searching for." Flynn said to the clerk.

As Flynn stepped nearer, closing the space between their bodies, the earthy, green scent of him enveloped her like an invisible cloak; triggering the memory of the first time he had entered her home and her heart, charging them both with the static electricity of his presence. When Flynn took her elbow, leading her away from the counter, a whisper of hope rooted in her soul. She longed to recapture the first stir of emotions she had felt on that day which now seemed like a lifetime ago.

So much had passed between them since that time—pleasure, pain, love and despair. Echo had clung to each emotion, no matter how unpleasant. She could not release them, or perhaps it was that they would not release her. Because she found herself suspended in an emotional limbo, she went willingly with him, hoping his reappearance in her life meant she might be able to find closure. Flynn guided her down the aisle, his polished shoes making a tapping sound as they glided across the marble floor.

Echo followed along with trepidation. They had not left things on a good note when they parted. Now the space between them was filled with all of the things they had and hadn't said to one another.

She wondered what he wanted with her now. He had vanished like a ghost, leaving all the unresolved issues between them in his wake. Had he returned to heal the wound, as he had once bandaged her bleeding skin, or was he here to drive the blade deeper yet? The prospect of having more accusations flung in her direction left a bitter taste in her mouth.

"I believe, miss, that we will find what you are seeking in the second floor stacks." Flynn announced too loudly.

The librarian shook his head, and turned his attention to an elderly man counting out change for overdue fines.

Through her peripheral vision she studied him. His body language was relaxed, but his face betrayed no hint of his current state of mind. There were so many things that she wanted to tell him, but realized now that she hadn't the faintest idea where to begin.

Unable to gauge his mood, she bit her tongue, restraining the phrases that threatened to spill from her lips. I love you. I need you. Please do whatever it is that you need to do to make things right again. Before she wore her heart on her sleeve, she would allow him to have his say, even if his words stung and wounded.

Wordlessly, Flynn led Echo up the winding iron staircase to the balcony above. Down below, people were scattered about at long wooden tables; their heads bowed over books and periodicals. A poorly clothed vagrant, escaping from the cold, snored loudly in a corner chair.

Winding through towers of dusty reference books, Flynn pulled Echo by the arm until they reached a far, dark corner.

"Miss me?" he asked.

The torment of missing him had been like the persistent phantom pain of an amputated limb. It nagged at her day and night, reminding her of what used to be. But the fear of his rejection and her damned pride floated, unseen but ever present, over her like an ominous specter. It whispered to her unconscious; *don't let your guard down.*

"What if I did?" She replied curtly.

"Still cheeky, I see." Flynn inched closer, crowding Echo against the wall.

Echo tested the waters, "Long time, no see."

"Yeah, well, after you said that you didn't want to see me ever again, I took your advice and went back home for a while. Not home like to my house. I went back to where I'm from."

Echo's guilt rose in her throat and it tasted bitterly of bile.

"Ireland?" she asked. "Around there, yes," Flynn replied. "Actually, I wasn't planning on returning here, but I was sent back to finish something I had started."

Echo tried to hide her disappointment. It was business that brought him back and not her.

He placed his hands on the wall on either side of her head, boxing her in. "Are you here on a research project, or have you decided to finally read all of the classics that you've always said that you wanted to read, but never had the time?" He smiled. "I can see it now, all curled up on the sofa in flannels, a cup o' tea in your hand, just you and a bloody good book. I suppose that next you'll be needin' to get yourself a cat or two to keep you company." His eyes studied her, making her feel small and vulnerable. "If so, I saw this grand orange pussy walking big as you please down the middle of the street."

"You have the nerve to call me cheeky?" The ice melted from Echo's voice. It felt like before; him teasing her, she feeling flustered in a flattered sort of way. The air seemed to literally spark and crackle when Flynn was around. He was a force of nature impossible to predict, and sweeping everything in his path along with him. He stood so closely, his intoxicating scent made her swoon.

She needed to apologize. She had to explain. She opened her mouth to speak but Flynn gazed into her eyes with his mystical blue orbs and she was speechless. The errant lock of hair that she had loved so much was hanging over his eyes. Echo reached up and smoothed it into place with her fingers.

"Lord in heaven, girl, I've missed you!" Flynn gasped, pressing his mouth to hers.

The icy exterior that had frozen her in its grip melted instantly with the warmth of his words. He had yearned for her; perhaps as desperately as she had yearned for him. Was it possible that he, too, had spent the last few weeks feeling like only half of a whole?

Echo tasted his lips and welcomed his tongue with hers. It was as if she were welcoming life back into her body; a body that had simply been going through the motions of living.

When he left, she had dug a shallow grave for her heart and buried it away. His kiss resurrected it from the dead, and it hammered like a fist upon her chest.

Her fingers glided through his hair. After all of the long, lonely weeks, she wanted to touch him, to feel his flesh, to know for certain that he was real.

The heat and pressure of his erection pushed against her abdomen.

"Care to come out and play for old time's sake, or are you going to cast me and this polecat in my pants out into the bitter cold?" Flynn asked.

Echo was stunned. Did he mean right here, and right now? She had carried the guilt of their failed affair with her for so long, and here he was, acting like it was all water under the bridge. Was this his way of granting them both amnesty from the past?

"Before you answer, let me plead on the polecat's behalf. The cold does not agree with him at all, you see." Flynn breathed into her ear." He prefers a climate that is a bit more... tropical." Flynn's hand slid under Echo's skirt.

Echo knew that if she allowed him, Flynn was capable of transporting her almost immediately into a state of wanton desire. She wanted—no— she needed him to know that he was more to her than just a good lay. The tables had turned. Now she felt like talking and he wanted to fuck.

"A hot, sultry location is more to his liking. So what say we send him on a balmy little holiday?" Flynn unzipped his pants.

"What are you doing?" Echo asked.

"Isn't it obvious? Just being near you and I'm out of control again. Echo, I don't care about what happened in the past. I'm desperately sorry for the things I said and did. I want to make it up to you if you'll let me."

His fingers caressed her pussy beneath her skirt and it responded with a warm rush of lubrication. He had forgiven her, but could she find forgiveness from herself? Her dishonesty and petulance had been a major source of the conflict and she needed to explain, to offer her own apology. "Will you let me make it up to you?" Flynn's finger slipped inside her panties and petted the wet folds. Echo buried her face in his neck. Yes, she yearned for him, it was true. But it was more than that. He had been callous in his accusations, but he had also been insightful. She was selfish, taking and taking without as much as a fleeting notion for his needs. He had done so much for her, had pleased her in so many ways. If a moment of make-up sex was what he wanted, it was the least she could do to mend the sorrow.

Flynn reached behind her buttocks and pulled her left leg around his hip. Without thinking, Echo placed her right foot on one of the bookshelves to steady herself. Several volumes on the other side of the bookcase crashed to the floor with a thud. The faces at the tables below looked up in unison. Seeing nothing out of the ordinary, they shrugged their shoulders and resumed reading.

"Shhh! This is a library. They'll revoke your card, and then what are you going to do on those long, lonely nights?" Flynn teased.

Flynn tore open a condom wrapper with his teeth and rolled the sheath over his erection. Echo opened her mouth to protest, and then remembered that they had been apart for weeks. A condom was probably a good idea. Hooking a finger inside of her panties he moved them to one side and entered her. It was as if a key had been turned, unlocking a secret bond between them. Beyond the physical sensation of his body joining with hers, it seemed that their two souls, which had been cleaved into halves, now joined to form a new, more complete union. All of the despair, regret, and longing she had clung to whistled through her body like a tempest. The raw strength of the emotions was so overpowering that she could scarcely bear it. Her heart swelled like a balloon, threatening to burst from the beauty and tragedy of their love.

Flynn, too, seemed moved beyond explanation. They stayed perfectly still like that, one inside the other, for what seemed like eternity, their breath marking time. A tear fell from her cheek, staining Flynn's shirt.

"Don't cry mo cuisla." He whispered. "It's alright, Flynn's here."

At a snail's pace, Flynn worked his shaft in and out of her. The movement was imperceptible except to the two of them. He did not kiss or fondle her. She was locked into his gaze in a mesmerizing visual fuck. Everything they hadn't said to one another was being communicated through their eyes; the regret, the sorrow, the love. Echo felt as if he was looking into her very soul, coaxing all of her secrets from her.

She tightly shut her eyes, afraid to let him in—afraid of what he would find.

"Look at me." Flynn said pushing his prick into her and pinning her against the wall. "Look...at ....me. Look into my eyes, Echo, and tell me that you don't love me. "

Urgently trying to control her impending orgasm, Echo's right hand flew out to grasp the edge of a shelf, toppling volumes of Byron and Browning to the floor. It was too late. Her vaginal muscles tightly gripped Flynn's cock as she quivered and climaxed.

Flynn kissed her mouth, softly, like a lover. Echo felt his vulnerability;

it poured into her mouth like bittersweet wine until it no longer belonged only to him, but washed over and through her until she too owned it. It wasn't a sympathetic, but rather an empathetic sensation so intense that it caused her head to whirl in a woozy fog. It was disorienting, as if she had no sense of herself as a separate being apart from him.

The desire to submit completely and utterly to him was so intense that she feared she would lose herself to him, following him blindly with no will of her own, like some pathetic zombie woman. It was too much. Even though her heart cried out for him, she felt a compulsion to break away lest she get swept up entirely.

Echo's feet found the floor, and she pushed Flynn backward, leaving him to stuff his unsatisfied erection back into his pants.

No one had ever caused this inexplicable reaction in her. The overwhelming intensity of the feelings she experienced when he was inside of her seemed different than they were before. They were frightening now in a way they hadn't been before. She had the sensation that she was a fly lured by fascination into a beautiful and mysterious spider's web that grew ever more tangled each moment she spent with him.

As much as she felt a compulsion to, she just couldn't surrender to him. It wasn't Flynn she didn't trust. It was herself she couldn't trust.

"I don't love you! I can't love you!" She hissed, hoping that in saying the words she could convince herself that they were true. She knelt trying to gather up the spilt books which only slipped from her arms and down to the floor again.

"Damn it!" she exclaimed, kicking the books with her toe.

Flynn grabbed her arm. "Echo, what is wrong?"

"Go away from me, Flynn. Do us both a favor and stay away from me."

"That's my point, Echo. I am going away. After tomorrow night, I have to leave. I want to take you with me, if you'll go."

Leave…he was leaving again? Echo's head began to swim. Here he was, once more springing a surprise on her at the last minute.

"This is not a schoolyard game that you are playing. I am not like one of the meek, mewling men that you have toyed with in your past. I can take it, Echo. Whatever you think you can dish out, I can handle. And I can love you if you let me."

Echo barely heard what he was saying. All that raced through her mind was, *he's leaving… he's leaving.* Isn't that what she wanted? Even as the thought crossed her mind, she knew it wasn't. The lyrics from a silly old song reverberated through her brain; *ever have the feeling that you wanted to stay, and yet that you wanted to go?*

"H-how long will you be gone?" Echo stammered. "I won't be coming back, Echo. I wasn't meant to stay here forever— this was only a temporary arrangement." His gaze drifted to the floor taking Echo's heart with it. He was leaving—permanently?

"Tomorrow is the last night. The Halloween party is my send-off. I want you to come with me. I won't pressure you for your answer right now, but at least say you will come to the party and think about going back with me." His gaze climbed up her form until it rested upon her face. The intensity, the importance of the decision which faced her made her feel both warm and cold.

"I have something very important that I've wanted to tell you for a long time. Please say you will come and just listen to me. You can make your decision after that," Flynn implored.

Echo wrestled with everything she was hearing. Her stomach tightened into a fist. Tears choked her throat. She didn't want to make this decision. She didn't want to make any decisions at all. In her present agitated state, she knew her judgment couldn't be trusted.

Flynn clutched her arms, shaking her. "Think, Echo. Think back on what you told me that you wanted from life—to love and to be loved. It's just that simple. Say you will come."

But it wasn't that simple. Their love had a cost she wasn't certain she was willing to pay. She wasn't the same person she had been before they met. Gradually, inexplicably, he had changed her. She had never guessed that living out her fantasy would have so many implications. What had started out as a game had turned into a life-altering journey. They couldn't go back the way they had come…to the way it was before they had started the game. She knew she would crave the delicious pleasure of his domination and seek to recapture those feelings at every turn. She was torn between the demanding desire to submit and the fear of it.

"I don't know, Flynn, I don't know. Maybe…..maybe, okay?" Peeling his hand from her arm, Echo rushed down the aisle without a backward glance, disappearing behind a soaring wall of books. Flynn pounded his fist against the window frame and watched through the glass as dried, broken leaves hurtled to the ice-covered ground below.

* * *

Bewildered, Echo shielded herself from the howling October wind that pushed through the open library door. Shivering with cold and confusion, she gazed at the bleak, grey sky.

Just when she thought she might be able to go on without him, he had shown up and fucked with her heart again. He had reignited the feelings between them and now he was leaving for good. What was she supposed to do with this information?

"Excuse me, miss. I think you dropped this."

A dirty hand held a small book out to her. Echo recognized the vagrant that had been napping in the library. She dismissed him smartly. She was in no mood for crazy today. She was already stocked up.

"No, you are mistaken. That's not mine."

"Pardon me, miss, but I saw you drop it. And, look, you even marked a page with this party invitation." The man opened the book to where a single piece of white card stock marked a passage.

Echo was about to disregard the vagrant again; then she saw it—the invitation from Flynn stared at her from the printed page. How could this possibly be? That wasn't her book.

She looked back towards the library. It would be just like Flynn to set this up and then be lurking around, watching her reaction. He probably paid the man to bring it out to her. He knew it would freak her out enough to leave a lasting impression. But for some inexplicable reason he must want her to be in possession of this book.

"Oh yes, that is my book after all," she lied. "Thank you for bringing it to me."

"It's okay." He placed the book in her hands. "Would you happen to have some spare change? I sure could use a cup of coffee."

"Sure, sure," said Echo, digging in her purse. "Here's a ten. Get yourself a hot meal too." The drifter nodded in gratitude, and shuffled into the driving wind.

* * *

At home, Echo carelessly threw the book on her bed and showered the scent of Flynn from her body.

With every cell of her being, she wanted to be with him. Yet, knowing that she depended on him so completely for her happiness put her in a place of such great vulnerability that it frightened her.

She wondered if he could be her Master. She wondered if she could submit to him enough to allow him that place in her life.

Could she be with him, submit to him and still retain the essence of who she was? Or by submitting would she lose herself? Was it possible that in submitting to his direction she would find a new way of being, so that she could settle into a peaceful coexistence with him, where she no longer struggled with the notions of independence that had been so strongly imprinted on her brain?

As she massaged shampoo into her hair, she sighed. It had all seemed so simple—a fun and exciting foray into forbidden pleasure. She had never imagined that it would affect her so deeply, that it would seep into every aspect of her life. The memories of their time together rolled through her mind once again. Those few hours when she had been able to drop her guard, and just be in the moment with him were pure delight. So why couldn't she feel like that all of the time? Why did she struggle and fight it so? When she was in his arms, she was filled with a sense of security and protection. When she wasn't in his presence, she felt the lure of him clutching at her like a captor.

The connection between them today had been all-consuming. She feared it might swallow her up entirely. It had spooked her so thoroughly that she hadn't even apologized to him. He had given her the perfect opportunity to tell him how she felt, and her damn angst and pride wouldn't allow it. She had even denied her love. Shame at the remembered cruelty of her words crept through her and settled into her being. No wonder he thought she only wanted his body. Her behavior in the library had illustrated that to perfection.

He was leaving. He hadn't even told her exactly where they would be going if she went with him. But did where really matter? Did anyone ever know where they would end up? Plenty of couples sacrifice the life they know for the relationship. In the end, all that matters is that they are together.

The doubts in her mind had nothing to do with whether she loved him or not. She had thought on nothing else for weeks. That she loved him was the only thing she was certain of. But did she love him enough to lay down her self-importance and apprehension—to put her heart into his hands and risk everything for him?

Could she give him what he needed? She wasn't certain that she even knew what he needed. Hell, she hadn't ever thought to ask. What did he obtain from her submission? He wasn't by nature the tyrannical type. It was clear he preferred to spoil her with kindness rather than punish her.

There was no cruel streak that ran through his bones, and he certainly didn't need a woman groveling at his feet to feel like a man. He possessed more masculinity in his little finger than many men had in their entire bodies. So what, after all, did he need from her?

Freshly showered, she sat on her bed and held the book in her hands. It was a collection of poetry by Alexander Pushkin. Echo slipped her feet under the cool sheets, opening the volume to the marked page.

No, never think, my dear, that in my heart I treasure
The tumult of the blood, the frenzied gusts of pleasure.
Those groans of hers, those shrieks; a young Bacchante's cries
When writhing like a snake in my embrace she lies,
And wounding kiss and touch, urgent and hot, engender
The final shudderings that consummate surrender.

How sweeter far are you, my meek, my quiet one.
By what tormenting bliss is my whole soul undone
When, after I have long and eagerly been pleading
With bashful graciousness to my deep need conceding,
You give yourself to me, but shyly, turned away.
To all my ardors cold, scarce heeding what I say.
Responding, growing warm, oh, in how slow a fashion
To share, unwilling, yet to share at last my passion!"

Echo read the poem again. A realization dawned in her mind. The verses spoke of surrender. He didn't just want her body; he wanted her heart and her soul, entrusted to him willingly. He needed to be needed. He needed her to recognize that he was strong and dependable, and protective. It was the essence of his manhood.

He loved her best when she yielded to him and she had been bucking him at every turn, selfishly thinking only of herself, relying on her own judgment and never truly giving herself wholly to him. Flynn was standing with open arms, waiting to embrace her willing surrender. Her heart awakened to the confirmation that this wasn't a game that could be played with and forgotten. It was an all or nothing proposition.

A Celebration of Submission

"Hey Flynn," King Arthur called out, "There's a naked girl kneeling on your porch!"

Flynn, who was brooding in the corner, looked towards the door in alarm. A naked girl…could the guests be that drunk already?

Flynn pushed his way through the crowd of costumed revelers and made his way to the door.

Nude, with hands bound in front of her, Echo knelt, shivering in a skiff of snow.

She had come! His heart sang, victorious at the sight of her. Perhaps a little too victorious—he hadn't asked her for this extreme demonstration. He had only hoped she would consider his invitation and give him one last chance. His eyes drifted to her hands and the red satin ribbon that bound them.

"Jaysus, Mary and Joseph," Flynn muttered under his breath, "I've created a monster."

Well, she certainly knew how to make an entrance. What in the hell can she be thinking, coming out in this blasted weather naked as the day she was born?

"Stand up, lass," said Flynn, whipping off his black satin cloak and wrapping it around her shoulders. "It's cold enough out here to freeze the balls off a brass monkey!"

Masked faces craned their necks around corners to stare at the unclothed woman trembling in the frigid air. Someone shouted, "Alright! Flynn hired strippers!"

Christ, how am I going to handle this one? He had to act fast; a crowd was forming.

"Don't be daft lad." said Flynn, thinking on his feet. "Can't you see this girl thought this was a birthday party, so she came in her suit? Now make way, so I can get this creature out from the cold!"

He didn't give a tinker's tit what the guests thought. He was so thrilled that Echo had arrived, even if she had done it in a very unconventional fashion, that his usually steady hands were trembling with the earthquake of his excitement. When she left him at the library yesterday, his hopes of ever seeing her again had crumbled. Now his despair was washing away as the hope of renewal sprang in his chest. The worry that had lined his face gave way to a broad smile, which he was powerless to subdue.

He rubbed her arms briskly with his hands. She was icy cold. He needed to get her through the crowd and into his room where he could warm her up, and he had to find out what was going on in her head. The curious throng parted. Their eyes followed Echo as Flynn guided her down the hallway and up the staircase to his bedroom.

Locking the door behind them, Flynn motioned to the low stool. "Sit," he said.

This woman was more dramatic than he was. All in all, he thought they made quite a pair. He wondered whether she was trying to shock him, or whether she was making some other statement that he was at a loss to understand.

Echo sat on the stool, her eyes lowered. The blood red ribbon contrasted starkly against her blue-white flesh. Flynn drew a small knife from his pocket and cut the ribbon, freeing her wrists.

Stepping back, he ran his fingers through his hair, shaking his head in disbelief. Echo had not uttered a single word, or even raised her eyes.

"Have you lost your mind, girl? What's this all about?" Flynn gestured at her nakedness, only partly covered now by his cloak.

Echo remained silent, her cheeks flushing red and her lip quivering. Flynn recognized the signs. She was on the verge of tears...again. Lord help him, what had he done to her? He got down on one knee and lifted her chin, forcing her eyes to meet his.

"Are you on drugs? What is it? Speak to me, Echo!"

Echo's eyes met his. There was such a look of sadness in them that Flynn could scarcely bear it. A leaden oppression, with the immovable weight of a stone monolith descended on him, suffocating his heart. This was her farewell scene.

"The invitation said, explore your innermost desires, and to dress accordingly. This is what I desire—to kneel before you, stripped of everything I used to be."

The sound of laughter filtered up the stairway. Echo glanced over at the door.

"Forget about them," Flynn said dismissively. "Right here...you and me ...that's all that matters." Once he had her full attention, Flynn was able to probe further.

"So, you think I want you to kneel to me? Naked as a newborn?"

"It's symbolic, Flynn...symbolic!" She rolled her eyes.

"Symbolic...yes ...of course...I see that now." He had a vague notion of what she was getting at, but didn't want to engender any further frustration from her by demonstrating his ignorance. Why couldn't women be more like men and just say what they meant? As long as he lived, Flynn decided that he would never understand women—especially this one.

"I wanted to show you that I come to you willingly, open and without pretense. I bound my hands in a symbol of submission to you. I couldn't think of any other way to tell you that I love you and if you'll have me, I will go anywhere you go."

All the cells in his body sprang to life as if his whole self had broken out in a joyous song. She was going with him! All he had really needed was to hear her intention, not this grand ill-conceived gesture. Flynn took Echo's cold body in his arms.

"Echo...Echo, I didn't need all of this. I just need you, lass. I've been brooding all night at my own party because you weren't here."

A loud crash came from the floor below, followed by the shattering of glass.

His guests were tearing up the place, but he ignored them and rained kisses onto Echo's frozen face. She was far more important than some broken crystal that he wasn't even going to care about after tonight.

Flynn released Echo from his arms and arranged the thin cape around her, tucking it under her legs to keep it from slipping. His cheeks ached from the smile that beamed across his face. But Echo wasn't smiling. She sat with her head bowed and her eyes cast downward. The air around her was heavy and thick. Flynn took her hand in his, blowing warm breath onto her frozen fingertips. "What is it? Is there something troubling you?" Echo eyed him, nervously chewing her lip. A few snowflakes still clung to her rusty hair.

"I want to say I am sorry, Flynn. I have wanted to tell you for weeks. I made a mess of things and I hurt you. I was afraid you wouldn't like me anymore if you really knew me."

So that's what she was agonizing over. She had been bearing the guilt of their spat for all of these weeks and he had run like a coward, leaving her to wallow in misery and self-doubt. He was constantly finding himself in the role of a cad in this mortal realm. Communication was a problem here and words weighed him down and tripped him up. It was so much easier back home, where telepathic communication left little room for misunderstanding. He should have reassured her that he hadn't expected perfection. He certainly was far from it. He only wanted her to trust him with her secrets. He didn't care what they were; he loved her in spite of them and because of them.

"Like you? Mo Chuisle, what I feel for you is so beyond liking. But I do like you too—most of the time." Flynn grinned and winked at Echo, trying to make her laugh. She didn't.

The corners of his mouth began to twitch as the smile faded from his face. "Come on, baby, you know I'm crazy about you. Who needs perfect? Perfect is boring, right?" He wrapped his arms around her shoulders. She seemed so small and fragile in her nakedness. "It's okay. Whatever it is, you can tell me. What is it that weighs so heavy on your mind? Give it to me and I'll carry it for you."

Echo took a deep breath. Uh oh, this one looked like it might be a doozie. For a second, Flynn thought she might be pregnant. It had been three weeks since their first time. There was a slim chance. In his blinding passion he had neglected to take precautions. So what if she was? It was okay by him. He wanted to have babies with her—lots of them.

"I hear voices…well, not lately, but all of my life. I hear voices from… from another dimension. I'm a clairaudient."

Echo winced waiting for his reply. His shoulders dipped, momentarily disappointed that she wasn't pregnant. He already knew about her clairaudience, but he had planned to discuss that and other matters with her after the party.

"Aw, is that all? That's nothing to be ashamed of."

Echo's wide-eyed look and slackened jaw communicated her astonishment. A pang of guilt stabbed at Flynn's chest. He shouldn't have let her worry over this secret. He should have found a way to let her tell him before this.

"It doesn't freak you out?" Echo asked

Flynn put his hands on either side of Echo's face. He looked her straight in the eye. "I don't give a fiddler's fuck whether you hear voices, see visions, or caterwaul in your sleep. All I know is that I met this girl named Echo Sullivan; she shook my hand and stole my heart. That's good enough for me."

Finally, the worry that had tortured Echo's face vanished. The dullness faded from her eyes and the light of life now sparkled behind her glittering green irises. Her cheeks blushed like dewy rose petals against the ivory creaminess of her skin.

Flynn could hear the Chicken Dance playing on the stereo downstairs. Someone had found his antique conga drums and was pounding out a crazy beat on them.

"I have some things I need to tell you too, but for now, they will have to wait."

"So, you're not angry with me for showing up like this and ruining your party?"

Flynn scratched his cheek nervously, as his brogue rolled off his tongue with charm. "No, lass, I'm not angry, in fact I am exceedingly moved. You're not ruining the party…you're the reason for the party! I was wallowing in complete and abject misery, certain that I would never see you again. But here's the thing, right now I have sixty guests downstairs, and a naked girl upstairs. Do you see my dilemma?"

Echo raised her eyes to his. He winked and tickled her waist. She giggled and slapped at his hands, wriggling instinctively away from his probing fingers.

Flynn was much relieved to see her back in good spirits. Now he truly felt like getting his party on. There was time later to continue this conversation.

"Behind that door over there, you will find something to wear that's a bit more suitable for public viewing. I bought it for you after our little rendezvous in the Halloween shop. I was waiting for the right time to give it to you, but…well, never mind… you're here now, so that's all that matters. Put it on. I'll be watching for you to come down the stairs."

"I couldn't go back and face those people. Please just let me stay up here until they are gone!" She pleaded.

It wasn't worth continuing with the party if she wasn't coming down to enjoy it. He wanted to celebrate their last night here and he wanted to do it with her by his side.

"I understand that you're embarrassed, but, believe me, you needn't be. That gang of drunken degenerates downstairs has no room to pass judgment on anyone. Every last one of them is wild as a March Hare and that's precisely why I invited them. I sincerely doubt you are the first naked girl they have ever seen at a party.

I want you to be with me and I want us to have a wonderful, unforgettable time. I can't do it without you. We're a team." Flynn held his hand out, palm up and Echo slapped her hand on his in agreement.

"Don't be troubled, girl. This is my house and these guests are here at my pleasure." Flynn removed the cloak from Echo and placed it on his shoulders. "If anyone snickers…I'll bite them!" He dramatically whipped the cape over his face in Bela Lugosi fashion. "Don't dawdle. I can't wait to show you off. We are going to have a banging good time!" His cloak billowing behind him, Flynn whooshed out the door.

Echo warmed her frozen body by the crackling fire for a few moments, screwing up the courage to face the party downstairs. The tension that had permeated nearly every aspect of her life had vanished and had been replaced by a feeling of renewal so exhilarating that her feet danced with joy on the carpet. She felt lighter than air. Through her nakedness, she had thrown off the mantle of fear and mistrust that had imprisoned her for too long. It was this seemingly absurd act that had allowed her the freedom to cleanse her soul and bare the secrets that had lain hidden in its depths.

The person she had been just a few hours before was just a memory now. In her place was a woman who was no longer confused by the love she felt…a woman who was willing to give as well as receive. A rush of serene contentment, more warming than the fire which toasted her fair skin, washed through her. The secure knowledge of their love for one another held her in its reassuring embrace. Her eyes, which had been cloaked in gloom, now looked out upon the world with the light of redemption.

She had made the soundest decision that she had ever made in her life and it felt fabulous. She realized that she was not in the least ashamed. She was proud and exceedingly joyful that she belonged to Flynn. He was the most magnificent, dynamic, and charismatic man that she had ever known. Any woman would be a fool if they did not adore him. In fact, Echo was certain; any woman would give their very soul to kneel nakedly before him.

With resolve, she walked to the closet and flung open the door. If Flynn wanted her by his side, she would be there. The decision to swallow to her pride and joyfully join him at the party didn't feel the least like she was giving in. It was more of a giving out—a gesture of willingness to please him. She belonged to him and him to her. The clarity of this simple truth resonated like the clear song of a bell within her, and she knew without a shade of a doubt that she had made the right choice.

"I am going to take my rightful place next to my man; we are going to have ourselves one hell of a time tonight!" Echo announced to the clothing that was hanging neatly on the rod.

And then she saw it, the ivory leather fishtail gown, with the boning and the immodest lacing and zipper. The soft white kidskin mask which he had chosen for her at the costume shop dangled from a hook. Embroidered satin opera gloves, embellished with iridescent fresh water pearls, were draped over the gown. A jeweled pair of Christian Dior stiletto sandals sat upon the floor. Tucked inside of one shoe, something caught the light and glittered. She bent over and extracted a pink diamond slave bracelet.

After dressing, Echo examined her image in the mirror. The dress fit as if it had been sprayed onto her form. Her full breasts swelled over the top of the corset, like muffin tops bursting from a pan. Her tiny waist was pinched snugly by the dress and the roundness of her hips curved gently outward, a testimony to her womanhood. She turned her body to check out the view from the rear and was greeted with the sight of her bare bottom, peeking out from the criss-crossed lacings. Flynn had not provided any panties for her.

Why would he, she thought. *He had no idea that I would show up here without a stitch of clothing! Oh, well,* she shrugged. *It is what it is. Plus, my ass looks fabulous in this dress!*

Out the door she went, stopping momentarily to correct her posture.

Taking a deep breath, she raised her chin and struck a regal pose. She felt like a queen and her king was waiting.

One measured step at a time, Echo made her entrance, a graceful gloved hand holding up the hem of her skirt. One by one, heads turned to stare, Superman, The Blues Brothers, Marilyn Monroe, a leering "gynecologist". The hum-humming of the crowd ceased. An occasional clink of ice on crystal was the only audible sound. Even the music had stopped to mark her entrance.

Just remember, you are never going to see these people again after tonight, she told herself.

Echo scanned the crowd for Flynn's face. Her knees knocked

nervously together. She paused halfway down the stairs, and then she saw him.

Flynn pushed his way through the crowd, meeting her where she stood. He stretched out his hand to her. Trembling, Echo placed a gloved hand securely in Flynn's strong grip.

The moment her hand touched his, Echo relaxed. Flynn had an uncanny ability to make everything better. Echo was confident that he would handle this situation with style.

Flynn had never seen Echo looking more spectacular. His chest swelled with pride. She was his and he wanted everyone to know it.

Bringing her to his side, he faced the multitude, announcing, "Lads and lassies, I'd like you to meet Echo. I know you'd all like to get to know her..." Flynn pointed at the leering gynecologist. "Some of you would like to get her number."

Laughter broke out in the crowd. Flynn had successfully broken the ice.

"However, this spectacular creature is mine. Please make her feel welcome and if you don't, I'll kick your degenerate asses out into the snow!"

The revelers cheered and clapped as Flynn and Echo completed their descent down the stairs.

Flynn put his arm around Echo's small waist and navigated her through the crowd. She was beaming. Her beautiful face lit up like a thousand Christmas trees. Everything Flynn had waited for was coming to pass. He felt like dancing.

"Now start the music," he announced. "I am escorting my date to the dance floor. And make the tune what we Irish like to call, an Erection Set...nice and slow."

He guided Echo to the parquet floor in the drawing room. As they took their dance positions, Flynn caught a glimpse of Echo's luscious bare bottom peeking out from beneath the lacing of her gown. His mind flashed back to the time when Echo was bent over his knees and her apple-bottom writhed beneath his hand. His cock began to pulse to the rhythm of the music playing on the stereo.

His hand slid along her waist to the small of her back, the ivory leather cool and sensual against his fingers. Her body yielded to his lead.

Flynn piloted her expertly, with flawless, silky steps across the floor. They moved as one, turning and stepping in a sensual pas de deux.

Spinning in sharp turns, feet fitting together like parts of the same whole, Flynn turned Echo until she was lightheaded and giggling. She was an excellent dance partner who responded perfectly, never attempting to take the lead, but reading Flynn's moves as if they had danced together for a hundred years. For three minutes and twenty-three seconds, the world disappeared, and it was simply him and Echo dancing towards eternity. He wanted to make it special. This would either be the first or the last dance they would ever share.

The music ended with a crescendo and a hearty round of applause broke out from the crowd.

Flynn took Echo's hand and led her in a curtsy while he accepted the approval with a deep bow and swish of his cape.

"Has anyone seen Doctor Cuervo?" Flynn quipped, "Because I think I need an emergency transfusion!" With his signal, the party was back into full swing.

Flynn kept Echo by his side throughout the night, introducing her and showing her off like a shiny new sports car. Echo adored it. She felt like the luckiest woman in the world.

Too soon, the party wound down and they waved goodbye to the final departing guests.

Flynn leaned his back against the door, looking a little drunk and a lot handsome. Echo swallowed him up with her eyes. His disobedient hair was slicked back. Echo could see his muscles rippling under his tightly fitted shirt. The Dracula cape was still draped over his broad shoulders, making them look even more expansive. She loved this man. Without a doubt, she loved this man.

The Choosing

"Well, mo chuisla, that was grand, wasn't it?"

Echo smiled sweetly, "Yes. Oh yes, it was grand!"

Flynn dropped his head and sighed deeply. "I have something to tell you. And I think that you had better sit down." He motioned to a chair in the parlor.

This sounded serious. Another surprise. The possibilities swept through Echo's mind. What fresh hell was this? Was he married? Did he have a family back in Ireland? Had he changed his mind about taking her home with him?

Echo removed her mask so that she might see him better and lowered herself into the chair. Flynn paced nervously, his fingers combing through his hair.

"There is quite a bit that you don't know about me. It was unfair of me not to tell you certain things, but I had to know that you were truly committed to me…committed to us as a couple."

The trepidation that had coagulated thickly in her chest loosened, allowing Echo to exhale the air she had been holding in her lungs. His words dispelled the notion that he was married, and it didn't sound as if he had changed his mind. Still, it must be a whopper of a secret. Echo had never seen Flynn this uptight. He was always so direct, and now he was struggling to find the right words.

"I need to reveal something to you, something that may frighten you. It terrifies me to tell you because I may lose you all over again." Flynn turned his back, gazing out into night through the window. His face, reflected in the glassy surface, was pinched with worry. "I am not quite what I seem." He haltingly proceeded. "How should I put this?"

Echo's analytical mind furiously tried to piece together what he might be leading up to. What did she know about him, really? She never saw him go to work; in fact, he never spoke of work. He lived a moderately opulent lifestyle, despite the fact that he seemed to have no visible means of support. Was he in the witness protection program or something equally sinister? Echo's stomach knotted into a fist.

Flynn continued to stare out into the night.

"I am a bit *more* than meets the eye. I am not sure what your beliefs are about the supernatural…about beings that aren't quite human…"

What did he just say? Beings that aren't quite human? Did he think he was some supernatural being?

Flynn did have an uncanny way of knowing things about her; things he couldn't have known. He had appeared in her life like a phantom and, every time she saw him, he had nearly always taken her by surprise. Echo reflected on the first time they met and the immediate impact he had had on her. From the first moment she had felt as if she were under a spell.

Then there were his eyes that glowed and hypnotized like heavenly bodies behind his pitch-black lashes. And the voice—the one that had haunted her and foretold the very words that Flynn would speak… an eerie chill slid down her spine.

"Flynn, "she interrupted, "are you trying to tell me that you are a…a creature…like a *vampire* or something?"

Flynn turned from the window, the corners of his eyes crinkled with amusement. "A vampire? What makes you think I am a vampire?"

"Well, the costume, for one." Echo pointed a gloved finger at his cape. "And…other things—the mysterious way you have of coming and going…

"Heavens no, lass," Flynn protested. "I'm most certainly not a vampire. I just thought it would be good fun to dress like one!"

Echo rolled her eyes in relief, exhaling a long sigh.

"But I am not entirely human either."

Echo shifted nervously in the chair. Could this be a game he was playing, or was he deranged?

"Let me try to explain and be out with it. I realize that what I am going to tell you will sound astonishing and beyond reason, but try to keep an open mind. Many things are beyond reason and are still true nonetheless…your clairaudience for instance."

He was right about that. Echo knew with certainty there was a shadowy world beyond that which she could see—a world most people only speculated about. She had hidden her gift from the scoffing world, knowing that people doubted what they could not understand. But she had lived with reminders of the reality of that hidden world nearly every day of her life. Her Granny had believed in many superstitious legends; Fey people, fairies, banshees and goblins. She had cooed Echo to sleep with tales from the old country where wondrous magical beings abounded in the forests and hillsides. Echo was no stranger to the unknown and unexplained.

Flynn's countenance took on a serious expression. Echo was certain now that he was not playing a game. A tightness rose in her throat and she swallowed it down, nodding at Flynn to continue.

Flynn moved into the light. For a moment, he appeared to shimmer translucently, like a desert mirage. Wow, she must have drunk more than she thought. Echo blinked her eyes and he was solid again.

"I am from an ancient and immortal race of beings known as the Daoine Sidhe." He pronounced it Deenie Shee. "It used to be that all Celtic people knew of our legend, but we have fallen into a dim memory at best and a silly fairy tale at worst."

Echo couldn't believe what she was hearing. Her grandmother had told her the legend of the Daoine Sidhe—tall, handsome people who lived in a land beneath the waves of a great lake.

Echo had adored listening to Granny's tales of the fun-loving and carefree people. They were gods and not gods, but something in between.

She had told her not to be frightened of her "gift" because the Sidhe had given it to her when she was born with red hair. Echo had always considered that her Gran was just making it up to make her feel special.

Flynn continued, "We are much like you, but not always quite as physical as you see me here…I'll get to that part in a minute." Flynn looked questioningly at Echo. She could tell he was gauging her response. "Are you still with me?"

Echo nodded her head reassuringly.

"I've wanted to tell you about my world for so long, and I have so much to share with you, but time is ticking away, so I need to make this brief.

The Daoine Sidhe enjoy the same things as you do, eating, drinking, lovemaking, we have always taken a great interest in mankind. Before recorded time we inhabited the land that you now know as Ireland. We were driven out when the humans came with their weapons, brutality and greed for land. We settled into a realm of the Otherworld called Tir-na-nog."

Tir-na-nog? Echo had heard—no—she had seen that name before! Yes it was in her dream! There was a road leading to a place called Tir-na-nog.

Now she was certain Flynn wasn't making this up. It was impossible for him to know what had been in her dream.

"Echo, have you heard of people claiming that they have seen traveling spheres of light that hover above the ground, then are gone as fast as they appeared?"

"Yes," Echo replied, "Many times."

"Mortals reason them to be ghostly apparitions, but they are only the Daoine Sidhe passing through your realm. There has always been an exchange between Sidhe and humans. We are capable of taking on and maintaining human form when the circumstances are right. As you have already discovered, we are also capable of coupling with mortals. Children from the union of Sidhe and human are noble and heroic. Many of your great leaders were products of these couplings."

Flynn walked nearer to Echo. An odd humming vibration emanated from him and seemed to blend with her energy.

"In fact, Echo, you are descended from one of those unions."

"I'm what? Flynn, how is that possible? I am about as normal and flawed as any human could be." She protested.

"No, you aren't. You are so much more than you know. Your great-great grandmother on your mother's side was Sidhe."

"That…that would make my mother part Sidhe too?" Echo queried.

"That's right…and you too."

"Does she know?" Echo asked incredulously. *If this is true, why didn't she ever tell me?*

"Echo, why do you think your mother goes traipsing to far-flung corners of the world doing wonderful, selfless deeds to ease people's suffering? That deeply empathetic part of her is from the Sidhe."

She had never given a thought to how sweet and kind her mother was. It was just the way she was. Even in the face of adversity, her mother always had known how to say and do the things that healed the wounds.

"How did I never know?"

"How *could* you know? Why do you think your mother was so insistent that you take the house? Just a coincidence? Echo, there is no such thing as a coincidence. She wanted you to discover your destiny on your own."

Echo was suddenly sorry that she had not paid more attention to the history of her family. She had long ago chalked their tales up to the wild imaginings of a superstitious people.

"Now, I need to explain my existence as you see me here before you. Your gift of clairaudience is not a one way street. Picture it as an open door in your mind; things can come in, however things can also go out through that same door. Desires, for instance, can become so compelling that they take form and appear as beacons to the world beyond. You are more powerful than you realize. Your strong need, and your Sidhe connection, drew me to you. Your soul cried out to me and I wanted to become the man that you most desired."

Somehow, deep in her soul, Echo knew that every word he said rang true. She had desired a man exactly like Flynn. Her attraction to him was nearly magnetic, like two forces that were powerless to resist one another. She knew a bond with him like she had never known—and a love for him that was deeper than she had ever felt possible. Many men had tried to change her selfish ways, but none had succeeded; until now.

Flynn drew closer. Kneeling on one knee, he took her hand in his. His face close to hers, Echo realized that he *was* almost too beautiful to be real. She remembered the night in the pub and the jealousy she had felt because he had outshone everyone in the room, including herself.

"Echo, I am your desires made manifest." He explained. "What I am, you have created, and like creator and creation—no matter what the future holds—we are bound, each to the other…for eternity."

Echo's hands flew to her mouth, his words reverberating in her head like a phonograph record jumping over the same phrase over and over again…Bound for eternity…bound for eternity. How could they be bound forever when he was immortal and she grew older by the minute? He would always remain this way—young and handsome and full of life, while every day that passed would drain the vigor from her mortal body until she was dry and shriveled.

"I told you that I have to go home tonight. I would like to give you a glimpse of where I am going, if you'll allow me."

Yes, she wanted to know. She nodded in agreement, expecting him to produce a worn photo album filled with images of the mysterious Tir-na-nog, but instead Flynn crossed his hands in front of her face and slowly fanned them open.

The sound of a million humming bees filled Echo's ears. The room shimmered and gave way to a vision.

A vast green land of hillocks and white paper bark trees stretched out before her. At her feet lay a mossy path dotted with rings of saffron mushrooms. Coming towards her was a maiden, exceedingly beautiful and riding on an ice-white steed. It was the woman from her dream. A golden crown was on her head and a mantle of russet silk, bejeweled in stars of amber cabochons, fell about her body and trailed to the ground, rustling softly upon the earth as she rode. Silver shoes were on the steed, and a crest of gold bobbed on his regal head.

The beauty of the place was so overwhelming that it took her breath away. Her heart seemed to overflow, and Echo's eyes brimmed with tears of joyous rapture as she gazed into the vision.

Drawing near Echo, the woman said, "Delightful is this land and fairer than you have ever seen. With wild honey drip the forest trees. Fairy horses race the wind and a thousand voices will sing thee to your sleep. No pain or sickness, death or decay may find you here. Enter any way you wish, but you may not leave the same way you came in."

The scene began to flicker and fade. "No, come back!" Echo pleaded. She wanted to stay and stay in this place of fairy horses and honeyed trees. But all too soon she was returned to the stark reality of the drawing room, where Flynn stood watchfully over her. She wondered how he could bear being so far from this wondrous place.

"Did you like what you saw?" he asked.

"Oh Flynn," she exclaimed. "It was the most..." Echo struggled to find the words that properly described how she was feeling. "I...I can't seem...I'm speechless."

"I know. Believe me I do. And that was just a glimpse; the reality of Tir-na-nog is beyond a mortal's imaginings."

"What did she mean that I can enter any way I wish but I may not leave the same way that I came in?"

"If you choose it, on this most sacred night of Samhain, when the veil between this world and the otherworld is thin and allows beings from both sides to pass freely between the two dimensions, I can share my immortality with you and bring you with me to Tir-na-nog. You will have an eternity of learning. I will teach you discipline and structure. I will instruct you how to use your gift to listen to the earth, the seasons, and the animals and to ease you through the transition mentally and physically. It is only at this moment that I can offer this to you, after tonight, the opportunity will be lost."

Echo sat bolt upright in her chair, her mouth ready to blurt out, "Yes, yes, take me there with you!" But Flynn held his hand up, quieting her.

"Before you jump to your answer, I have to tell you that once you pass over, you will not be able to return here for a very long while. Time passes differently in my home and what passes in days there, passes as years here. Ultimately, with training, you will be able to move from one realm to the other, changing form at will, but, by that time, all you know will have gone from the earth."

So it was final. Once she made her mind up to follow him to Tir-na-nog, there could be no looking back, no saying goodbyes, just a silent slipping away into another world.

What was there to think about? Flynn offered her immortality in a land beyond description. What did she have here? A meaningless job, no friends? Her family was scattered across the globe and she hadn't seen them in ages. If she chose to remain behind, she knew that she would be staying alone.

Flynn paused, staring intently into Echo's eyes, his blue eyes now glowing with preternatural light. "I know I have given you a mouthful to chew on, but your decision needs to be made now. Make it from your heart, Echo and not your mortal head. I have to ask you again. Do you choose me for your Master?"

Echo rose slowly from the chair. She stood at destiny's fork in the road. If she turned left, she could walk out the door and back to her life. The path on the right led to Flynn and the vast unknown of eternity. He had given up, even if only temporarily, his life in the most wondrous place she had ever seen, just to be with her. Now, he was offering her the most tremendous gift he could possibly give, but what did she have of value to offer to him?

She gracefully picked up the hem of her dress. She stood before Flynn for a moment, wondering what she could offer him and she dropped to her knees and stretched out, prostrating herself at his feet. All she had to give was herself.

"I gratefully accept your generous gift and in return, I offer you the gift of my heart. I know you will cherish and protect it as if were your own. I offer you my life, which I trust you to honor, because you are a man of honor ,and you are steadfast and true. I offer you my undying love which asks for nothing in return, because it never has belonged to me—it was yours all the while."

Flynn placed his hand over his heart, willing it not to burst from his chest. Her love for him radiated outward, and the intensity of the emotion caused him to stagger backward a step. After all of this time, amid passion and tears, his dream had become reality. She had chosen him—above all others—she had chosen him.

Bending low, he took Echo's hand and guided her to a standing position. Her fair face was sweet with childlike trust and anticipation. Wrapping her in his arms, he kissed her mouth.

"Have I ever told you that I love you?" he murmured, his cheek pressed against hers.

"Never."

"I'm telling you now. I love you, Echo. I love from the tip of your toes to the depths of your Irish soul." Flynn squeezed her tightly, wanting never to release her from his embrace.

"Oh God, Flynn, I love you too. I love you so much it scares me."

Flynn glanced at the mantel clock that ticked away the magical minutes. There was less than an hour before midnight.

"Echo, we have to go. Samhain is nearly spent."

The Seed of Immortality

Flynn raced Echo down a steep, dark staircase ending at an arched wooden door, easily twice her height and bound in black iron. Turning the weighty bolt, Flynn pressed his body against the wood and it groaned open. A rush of warm air blew across Echo's face. Flynn beckoned her inside.

The room was black as pitch. With a wave of his hand, a multitude of niches carved into the stone walls illuminated with candle flames.

Echo was wide-eyed in amazement. Like a magician, Flynn had bent the laws of nature and called light into the darkness. Her Granny's words about the Daoine Sidhe came back to her—gods, but not gods, something in between.

The stone wall of the round room was etched in symbols, the meaning of which Echo could not grasp. On the floor, a pair of intersecting circles was drawn with a silvery powder. Just beyond the circles, a dense pile of exotic animal skins were heaped in an inviting pallet.

A curious wonderment overcame Echo. Were these the last things she was ever to see of this mortal world? She memorized the room with her eyes and tucked it into a pocket in her mind.

Flynn took her by the hand and led her into one side of the circle. "Are you ready?" he asked.

Echo nodded in agreement, her knees knocking in anticipation.

"Alright then, help me out of this get up," he said positioning himself in the opposing circle.

Echo thrilled. The thought of undressing Flynn caused an aching deep inside of her. Her pulse quickened as, with trembling, gloved fingers, she reached to remove his clothing. She slid the cape from his shoulders and it landed in an airy billow on the floor. She pulled his shirttails from inside of his waistband and meticulously unbuttoned the line of polished black buttons that ran the length of his torso. Her hands reached beneath the fabric, gliding along his muscular chest and slipping the shirt from his brawny arms. It was then that Echo noticed an ethereal glow emanating from his flesh. She felt her fingers passing through an invisible, but palpable field of energy as she knelt, removing his shoes and socks. She knew with certainty that she was in the presence of an immortal.

Flynn remained silent, looking down upon Echo as she looked up towards his belt buckle, his trousers straining with the girth of his impatient prick.

He groaned when Echo jerked the leather of his belt strap backward, tightening it briefly against his body before releasing the catch. When Echo dipped her fingers beneath his waistband to unbutton his pants she discovered the reason for the groan. The head of his cock lay strangled just behind the top of his trousers.

The tips of her gloved fingers skimmed the surface of his throbbing purple head as she unzipped him, releasing the pressure on his swelling behemoth. In a single tug, she freed him from the last of his clothing and he stood before her—his body a feast for her eyes.

His penis was larger than she remembered. Fully erect, the swollen head touched the top of his navel. It too, glowed with the same unearthly light as the rest of his body. Echo could see the veins beneath his skin pumping the blood into his monstrous prick. Her mouth watered at the sight of his straining cock and her hands longed to be rid of the gloves so that she could feel the silkiness of his rigid skin beneath her fingers.

"Echo, meet The Crippler" he said, showcasing his penis with his hands. *You've got that right.* Echo didn't know how they were getting to Tir-na-nog, but if he was going to use that on her, she sure wouldn't be able to walk there.

Reaching down, Flynn loosened the ties on Echo's gown. Her heaving breasts broke free from the corset. She longed for the sensation of his flesh against her flesh.

Touch me, Echo thought, Oh Flynn, please touch me.

His hand cupped her elbow, bringing her to her feet. Flynn tugged on the wide zipper that held the front of her gown together, and the dress collapsed to the floor.

Standing naked, Echo remembered what this was all about. She had gotten lost in the undressing and revelation of their bodies. She had momentarily forgotten that she was leaving this world for another—but how?

As if Flynn had read her thoughts, he explained. "From time to time during this transformation, I am going to have to perform a bit of magic mumbo-jumbo. Please try to take it seriously, Echo and show it the respect it deserves, alright?"

"I will...I do. I do take it seriously." She nodded her head reassuringly.

"Don't be frightened," he instructed. "Just do as I say and you'll be fine."

Echo wasn't frightened. She was crawling with the anticipation of a bride taking her first tentative steps down the aisle.

"Assume the upright kneeling position, your hands clasped in front of you."

Echo reverently knelt on the stone floor, her eyes respectfully downcast.

Flynn stepped out of the circle, his muscular buttocks like two ripe plums. He walked a few feet to where a triangular table balanced on three legs. He struck a match and put it to a bowl of black powder. The powder flared up quickly and then died down to ashes. He followed by placing an opaque golden stone into the powder. An intoxicating aroma rose in curling ribbons of silver smoke from the bowl. Echo filled her nostrils with the sweet, earthy scent. It reminded her of Sunday mass when the heavy aroma from the burning censers drifted over the heads of the congregation in the cathedral.

Flynn carried the bowl and stepped purposefully around the silvery circle. With his hand he wafted the smoke over Echo's kneeling form, reciting.

"I call upon the influence of frankincense and myrrh, your erotic powers on this servant to confer. Mingle your essence on Samhain night, as servant and master do here unite." Flynn observed Echo fall into a dreamy, nearly hypnotic state. Her shoulders relaxed several inches, and she filled her lungs with air in smooth, even inhalations. He reached his hand out, palpating the energy that surrounded her. The power of the ritual combined with the incense had lifted her to an elevated state of consciousness. Perfect. She would need to achieve a level where nothing existed but the purity of love—aware of what was happening around her, but vibrating to a frequency that more nearly matched his.

Setting the bowl on the floor, Flynn stepped inside of the entwined circle.

"Protected inside this circle of rings
The Sidhe of olde, immortality brings.
Ancient ones welcome and open the portholes,
Celebrate and bless the joining of two souls."

Flynn knelt, taking Echo's hands in his. He willed a tremendous outpouring of energy through his hands into hers, mingling their essence until two became one.

"From the powers below to the five archangels above,
I command you this night, bring new life to my love.
Release all that's been, release all that's old,
Wipe clean the past, let new life unfold.
Oh, powers that be, fling wide the door.
I bring with me a love like never before.
I will her home, at last, now with me,
And so it was written, and so shall it be."

"Look into my eyes, Echo" Echo raised her eyes. She wasn't sure if it was a trick of the smoke enveloping the room or if it was real, but there appeared to be two of Flynn; the flesh and blood Flynn and an iridescent, shimmering Flynn that emanated from his body. "In order for this transformation to be complete, we need to join together body, mind and spirit," Flynn explained. "The seed of immortality will only anchor and flourish where there is true and absolute love between two beings. Sidhe seed is sacred and not given on a whim. You will realize why I couldn't take the chance of ejaculating inside of you before this."

The knowledge that he was this close to possessing her caused Flynn's anxious prick to jerk at its root. "We have had sex before, but tonight we make love."

Gathering Echo into his arms, he lifted her body, and then settled it onto the animal skins that lay upon the floor. Her hair spread across the pillows like cascading boughs of bittersweet. Soon she would be with him in the land where the Daoine Sidhe ruled the dappled forests. The sexual energy they generated was a key ingredient to the transformation. But he mustn't let his impatience sully the moment. He would have to gently coax her to the increased vibratory state where there was an energetic pull between them; magnetism so strong that it could no longer be denied.

Flynn sat on the edge of the bedding, removing Echo's gloves. "There are only a few rules that you will need to remember." He instructed. "Number one, relax. When you feel your body tensing, bring yourself back to a relaxed state. It is very important that the energy is not concentrated specifically in your sexual organs but that it is allowed to spread over your entire auric field. Do you think you can do that?"

"I'll try." She smiled.

"You'll do fine, lass," Flynn reassured. "Secondly, remember to breathe. Don't hold your breath. It will help you to relax and focus. Last, but not least, enjoy what you are experiencing and try not to rush things. We have all of eternity to be as impetuous as we want, but tonight is not for that."

Relax, breathe, enjoy. Echo reminded herself. The air was thick with the spicy fragrance of the incense. Echo closed her eyes for a moment luxuriating in the aroma as she stroked her hands over the sensuous glossy furs lying beneath her naked skin.

Echo casually noticed that her faster-than-lightning mind had quieted to a low rumble. Gone were the nagging, persistent thoughts that normally raced in her brain. She observed Flynn's actions with a passive, detached curiosity.

Flynn ran his fingers along a high ledge. It was up here somewhere. Ah, there it was—a jewel-encrusted chest, the size of a small cigar box. Extracting a vial of amber oil, he measured three drops into his palm, warming it between his hands.

Flynn studied Echo's form. She was the portrait of perfection, her pale, perfect skin nestled in the velvety hides. Gone was the intense eagerness that usually defined her visage. Her face now bore a peaceful serenity. Her still-mortal eyes could not yet perceive the subtle change in her auric field, but he could. The once fiery flames of swirling vermilion and saffron were now a tranquil shade of aquamarine, shimmering softly around her form. The anointing would assist in raising the discharging energy from green to indigo, then violet, and finally culminating in the luminous white light of immaculate love that was necessary to complete the transformation.

Flynn began at her feet, working the oil onto the fleshy bottoms and between her toes. Her toenails, painted a glittering pink, resembled tiny seashells. He kissed each blushing digit one by one. They wiggled against his lips.

"Does that tickle?" he asked.

"Nooo," she cooed. "It feels wonderful." Echo langoursly stretched her legs, pushing her feet against Flynn's chest. She slid their soft, slippery bottoms over the muscled outline of his pecs, savoring the tactile sensation of his hairs gliding between her toes.

Flynn dripped more oil into his palms and massaged Echo's outstretched calves. His fingers worked deeply into her muscles which had been flexed for hours by her torturous stilettos. As his fingers neared the sensitive skin on her thighs, Echo's pelvis tensed with anticipation. Deliberately, she released the tautness, and melted into the fur that cradled her body. When she loosened the tightening, the pleasurable feeling was able to intensify and wash over her entirety. The whole of her body purred with awakening.

Flynn's touch was firm, yet tender; willing every last bit of tension from her legs which suddenly felt very heavy. What an unimaginable state of bliss this is, she observed. Until this moment, Echo's validation and fulfillment had come from their frenzied, heated coupling. Now Echo felt such a great outpouring of love that could only be satisfied by the ultimate expression of mingling her body with Flynn's. No longer did one plus one equal two; Echo recognized that one plus one equaled one.

Flynn knelt over her, lowering his head to place a kiss on her navel. Something tugged deeply on her spine, releasing a silvery wisp out of the small puckered depression. Echo's essence fused with Flynn's as he drank it into his lungs. Unexpectedly, she vividly discerned the very core of his being; compassion, strength, wisdom, joy…the intensity of Flynn's quintessence was overwhelming. Breathe, relax, enjoy. She placed her hands on either side of his head, his hair falling through her fingers like fine silken threads. She held him there, his cheek cradled against the soft pillow of her belly. At that precise moment, she knew with the utmost certainty that her soul had found its mate.

"I love you so much, Flynn," she crooned, stroking his hair.

Flynn raised his head and held his body over hers, pouring his heart into the still green waters of her eyes. "And I love you so much, too, Echo." He lowered his mouth to her ruddy lips and relished the warm, honeyed taste of her.

Echo's arms embraced his neck. They no longer clutched and tore at him in frantic desire, but held him to her body with the sweetness of surrender.

The swell of her breasts pressed against his chest. Flynn's manhood, which had relaxed into a comfortable tumescence, stirred against the smooth flesh of her thigh. Echo's manicured fingers slipped between their bodies and wrapped his prick. Her touch was ambrosia!

Flynn rolled onto his back. Tonight he would permit Echo to take the lead and dispense her own brand of magic on him. She cuddled into his arms, her legs entwined with his. He felt the dampness of her sex against his thigh. How Flynn had longed for this moment. Through eons of time he had charted his lonely course. Nothing left to do now but allow it to unfold as it should.

With weightless caresses, her fingers worshipped his flesh, pausing to admire each hardened muscle, each pulsing vein. Flynn's energy hummed beneath her gossamer touch. She moved her body over his. Raining salutations of kisses down his torso she whispered, "My Master...my Lord...my King."

Her utterances were more insightful than she knew, for Flynn was not only a Daoine Sidhe, he was a Prince of the realm, and reluctant heir to the throne of Tir-na-nog; a position that he had shied from until now. Her submission and admiration made him feel worthy of the title. If he had won this woman's love, he could do anything that was asked of him.

Echo knelt between his robust thighs, her copper locks cascading over her full, rounded breasts—a goddess of erotica. Flynn's manhood twitched with anticipation, the promise of her mouth, enticing it to full erection. The impatient monolith twitched eagerly for her touch. Bending low, her hair tumbling onto his flesh like a rushing waterfall, Echo summoned his cock into her mouth. Her aura, which only Flynn could perceive, surged with iridescent violet rays. The rapturous sensation of her tongue as it tarried over his engorged head, making long, languorous sweeps around the ridge, pausing to dip into the tiny cleft, coaxed morsels of nectar from his loins.

At the taste of his enchanted fluid, a tremor rippled through Echo. A vision flashed in her mind's eye; a great courtyard, surrounded by stone walls, yet open to the blue sky. Immense figures carved of malachite circled the enclosure, their faces handsome and fierce. A long table groaned beneath a banquet of fruits, fowl and smoked meats. A voice spoke in her ear. "Greetings from the court of the Daoine Sidhe, Princess of Tir-na-nog."

As swiftly as it had materialized, the vision evaporated and Echo was once again aware of her surroundings, the bewitching flavor of Flynn's elixir still on her tongue. Did someone just greet her as a Princess of Tir-na-nog? The enormousness of the gift Flynn was bestowing on her overwhelmed Echo with devotion to her Master. She wanted nothing more than to honor and serve him all the days of her life.

She took his silky shaft into her mouth, unable to swallow the full length of the colossus. Honoring Flynn with her lips soothed Echo's soul. Pleasuring him was her deepest desire, and she discerned her own desire thirsting in her loins.

Flynn bent his legs, opening them widely, and pushing his prick against her soft palate. Echo feared that she may choke and grasped his hardened shaft with her hand, using it as an extension of her mouth as she drew his magnificent member through her lips and back again. A groan of pleasure rumbled from Flynn's throat. Echo could not get enough of the taste of his cock. She loved filling her mouth with its demanding girth, grazing his flesh with her teeth as she pulled it from her lips and then gobbled it back into her.

Flynn's hands were on her breasts, lifting and pushing them together. Echo released his spear from her mouth with a slurp and guided it into the deep crevice of her cleavage. Flynn pumped his wet cock between her fleshy mounds. Echo watched his purple head play hide and seek over the blue veins of her tingling breasts. She imagined him splattering her neck with his preternatural load and she gasped.

"Flynn, please, let me make love to you now."

Flynn released her breasts and Echo climbed onto him, straddling his hips. Engaging his eyes with hers, she descended on his penis, encasing it in her steamy cockpit. Exquisite torture played across his face as he gritted his perfect teeth, sucking a long draught of air into his lungs with an audible hiss.

For a long moment, Echo held him tightly inside her, milking his shaft by clenching and unclenching her spongy muscles against the unforgiving rigidity of his Herculean staff. It was all she could do to refrain from riding him with wild abandon, plunging his length into her and pounding it against her womb.

Flynn gripped her buttocks and rocked her up and down the length of his cock. Echo cued to the pace, feasting on the sensation of his prick sliding over the slippery walls of her dank cave. She communicated her rapture with her eyes, never once breaking the connection of his gaze. Pulsating hues of peacock colors rippled over Flynn's body. Echo watched in awe as the jewel tones swirled in patterns of amethyst, citrine and emerald. This was more than a coupling; it was a cosmic joining of two souls. "It's time, Echo," Flynn sighed. "Close your eyes, lass and follow me."

Echo surrendered, her eyelids shuttering her vision. Flynn's finger circled her clitoris, anointing the firm pearl with her own lubricious juices. The consistent pressure of his skilled hands urged her toward gratification. A slap-slapping sound pounded in her ears and Echo realized that it was the reverberation of her hips against his as she bucked and rolled her body on Flynn's fearsome cock.

The fur beneath her legs suddenly felt more luxurious than before.

Echo detected each individual hair brushing against her skin. She swore she could hear drops of her own fluids falling from inside of her and landing with a soft splash on the pelt below.

A magnificent euphoria swept over her body. She felt herself rising into the air, being lifted by the wind. She relaxed and let the feeling consume her and, when she did, her body unleashed her orgasm. She wailed her satisfaction into the night; in the distance a warrior cry answered her refrain. A scalding heat blasted inside of her. Electrifying sparks zinged through her corpuscles, charging her nervous system with white hot energy.

She collapsed breathless, in a heap upon the furs, not daring to open her eyes. Comforting solar rays warmed her face. High above her head, Echo heard a wood thrush warbling a joyous melody.

"Echo," Flynn's voice floated in the air. "Open your eyes, darlin' and see where our love has brought you."

Echo risked peeking through her lashes. The dark depths of the stone room were gone, replaced by a luminous, golden light. Could it be true? Had she arrived at the place of her vision? Her curious eyes opened wide onto a scene of impossible beauty.

She no longer lay on the pelts of fur, but on a cool carpet of dense green moss inside of a dappled forest of hawthorn trees. In the distance, she spied cottages, their rounded roofs thatched with feathers of red, gold and blue. A rustling in the leaves drew her attention to a hornless stag. He spoke to her as the voices had once done, "Fair maiden, we have long awaited thee, for thy coming has been fated." With that, the red stag bounded across the path and vanished into the dense copse. Echo was astounded. She knew it was impossible, but she had actually heard the animal speak to her.

Echo sniffed the air, and it bore the same wild, fresh scent as Flynn. She sat upright, leaning back on her elbows. Turning to her left she saw him smiling his familiar, impish grin. The unruly lock of hair had tumbled over one eye. His naked, muscled body stretched out in satisfied repose in this strange place, like an untamed creature of the primordial woods.

"Well, mo chuisle, what do you think?" Flynn gathered her into his arms, covering her face with kisses.

What did she think? Living happily ever after in this wondrous world with her primeval prince was more than she could comprehend.

"I think," she paused looking into his sapphire eyes. "I think that eternity is a very, very long time."

"Ahhh yes, 'tis, lass, 'tis," Flynn replied, rolling on top of her.

"But think of the possibilities!"

The End

Latest titles from Black Velvet Seductions

Their Lady Gloriana by Starla Kaye
Cowboys in Charge by Starla Kaye
Holly's Big Bad Santa by Starla Kaye
Her Cowboy's Way by Starla Kaye
The Love She Wants by Mila Winters
Punished by Richard Savage, Nadia Nautalia & Starla Kaye
Accidental Affair by Leslie McKelvey
Right Place, Right Time by Leslie McKelvey
Her Sister's Keeper by Leslie McKelvey
Playing for Keeps by Glenda Horsfall
Playing By His Rules by Glenda Horsfall
Sympathy Dance by Sue McConnell
The White Spider of Savignac by V. L. Smith

See more of our titles at
www.blackvelvetseductions.com

Our titles are available from:
Amazon
Smashwords
LuLu
Nook
and other retailers

Find Black Velvet Seductions on Facebook

And follow BVS Books on Twitter

www.ingramcontent.com/pod-product-compliance
Lightning Source LLC
Chambersburg PA
CBHW030336020726
47493CB00004B/1294